TWURK & THANG:

THE INSEPARABLES
(Part One)

Acknowledgement

First, I would like to thank my Creator (God/Heavenly Father) who blessed me with prosperity through all of my trials and tribulations. People who gave me inspiration, to keep on believing in myself, I thank you! You made me believe that I an unsigned an unpublished author, deserved to be recognized. With this encouragement, I pursued the desire to be able to share my creative/ real life stories with the world. I've had my shares of ups and down. People reading my stories gave me the push I needed to press on. I have dreams of becoming a new trend setter, as well as give the people what they need and want. I hope to inspire many more people with this opportunity and manifest my future endeavors.

To everyone, I say, never give up nor stop believing in yourself and your dreams. We can visualize a fantasy to reality, you only have to just believe that you can achieve then you can do the impossible. I want to thank my agent, Deidra, who is always hard at work. Thank you for helping and believing in me. I thank my family! For you have stuck by me in the past, and still you're by my side. You have believed in me and believe in me still. I hope in due time I will become the successful author that makes you proud.

Signed,

Frank Ziegler Jr.
AKA
Frank Nitty
BKA
Ekunde Kweli

"Hearts For Inmates"
"Invite To Enlighten"

Hotep! Greetings & salutations to my fellow comrades, and to all men/women and boys/girls! First & foremost, today marks a very important day in our time and era. It is the moment to take time out of your busy schedules, and find out about "Invite To Enlighten" as well as what it has in common with "Hearts For Inmates". We, the incarcerated, have been enduring such harsh conditions, long extended bids, and have yet to receive any relief. "Hearts for Inmates", isn't just a name or a program that represents a false impression and broken promises. They are actually displaying their hearts by doing the work that's needed to be done. Many have talked the talk, less have walked the walk. It's time to step up and stand firm together, and let's collectively start a progressive and effective move/movement. My idea is: "Invite To Enlighten". Many may ask, "what exactly is the "Invite To Enlighten" movement?" Well, let me, the founder of "Invite To Enlighten" move/movement, and author of this new and highly anticipated release enlighten you. The purpose of the movement will be to bring US, as one mind, body, heart, and soul. As well as to take a pledge to stand UNITED with all my brothers and sisters. Be on the look-out for our "Invite to Enlighten" page as well as the author page that will be home to all my bodies of work.

-----O. G. Nitty

Shout out to Alex McDaniel for inspiring me to write this for the incarcerated!

Twurk and Thang: The Inseparables is born from the bond I share with my brother with the names coming from our childhood nicknames. My name being Twurk and my brother's, Thang. We were like Yin and Yang. In this series, you will see that Twurk is the brains/mastermind. Thang is all about that action first and talk later. My brother and I made a vow to stay together and never let anything or anybody come between our bond as brothers. In life things do happen and changes occur. Life will always stake its course but blood will always make us one.

I hope you enjoy my first release!

Chapter 1

"Knock! Knock! Boy, turn that damn music down! I don't know how you hear anything with all that damn music!" said a loving but frustrated mom in the midst of her morning ritual with her two sons. The bathroom door opened as one of them peered out of it and asked, "What's going on here?" "Oh! I'm glad to see that at least one of you are up!" she said with the frustration easily seen on her face. "What's going on?" he repeated showing some concern. " Boy, you and that twin brother of yours spitting images of your father. God bless his soul! You to have his height his weight his light brown skin and his athletic figure. On top of that, you have his eyes that change from green to grey. That is why I constantly tell you two that you better not try and turn this house into no damn daycare center!" She was always a straight shooter with them.

Twurk found it particularly funny and laughed nonchalantly. This only made her even more frustrated as she peered at him through her now squinted eyes. "So, you think this is funny? Go ahead and call my bluff then! I'll have the both of you sleeping in shelters!" Twurk seeing that she was serious gave her a look to attempt ease her tension. "Boy, don't look at me like that. That is the same look your father used to give me, which is why you two are here."

Thang finally came out of the room." You two talking about me?", he asked. Mom then turned towards Thang. " Yes! We were talking about you, but I was also trying to tell you that the music was entirely too loud!" she told him. "My two sons! I wish you father we're still here. He would be so proud to see what strong and handsome men you two have turned out to be." Her once frustrated face now adorns a smile.

"Mom, I am tired of hearing about him! He is not here, so can we let him stay dead! Cause all this talking about him is not going to bring him back. I need a shower and you two are blowing my fucking morning!" replied Thang. He then continued, "You know what? What happened to the "good mornings", the "breakfast is on the table" and keep it moving days? That is what the fuck I am missing!" Thang stared at them with an annoyed but smiling face while they in turn look at each other in disbelief. They couldn't believe he had just said all of this. Mom appeared to be hurt as her eyes began to water. She then turned to walk away while shaking her head.

"What the fuck you still looking at me for? Don't tell me I struck a nerve with you too twin bro?" said Thang with a cocky smile at the corner of his mouth. "If you did, best believe I wouldn't just be talking or staring at you. Believe that! And when you get that chip off your shoulder, you owe our mom an apology! ASAP!" said Twurk as he stepped out of the bathroom doorway. Thang then went inside only to slam the door in Twurk's face.

Twurk goes inside of Thang's room. He shook his head as he turned down the loud music. He saw a picture of him and Thang which caused him to reminisce on past days. It was a picture of them on their 18th birthday party. What also made this day special was the fact that it was also the day they were released from juvie after doing a 5 -year bid for drug-trafficking and manslaughter. The only reason they were spared a much harsher sentence had something to do with their dad's being a high-ranking Captain in the Army during that time. They spent most of their five years getting educated and prepared mentally, physically, spiritually, economically and socially. Their bond to each other was always solid and unbreakable. They're so much alike in many ways, except when it comes to their attitudes and approach. Twurk had always been the level-headed mastermind that would weigh the options, thinking the situation through and then come up with the best possible option that would win the war instead of the smaller battles. Thang was the type that will hurt or cause someone to get hurt, then things just will magically blow over. When it did, it was mostly because of Twurk's influence.

When Twurk and Thang were 12 going on 13, they were hustling for their very own father. This is something they never told their mom. One day they were moving a few packs as usual, when

Twurk got a bad feeling in his gut about the ride to the drop-off that day. He turns to Thang with a worried look on his face. "Yo bro, I got a bad vibe about this ride." Thang replies, "Fuck it! We go down. We go down together!" He obviously had no cares and disregarded Twurk's gut feeling. Their bond became even tighter and they were often known as "The Inseparables". The ride to their drop-off point was going smooth until out of nowhere they became surrounded by N.A.R.C.S.

"Freeze! Get your black asses out of the vehicle and on the ground!" the cop yelled over the bullhorn. They exited the ride after taking in the scene and seeing that there was no way out. They glanced at each other, hopped out the whip and started dumping hitting two police officers before they were on the ground laying in their own blood. Luckily their father told them about wearing vests so no vital organs were hit. Although this was a past memory, to Twurk, it seemed like yesterday. "Damn!" he said to himself. He inhaled and then exhaled deeply. This was a remedy he had been using since juvie to help him clear his mind in order to think clearly and rid him of anger. Twurk left Thang's room and went to his room. He lit an Indian-head incense as he observed the many sacred portraits of history's legends, whom he called forefathers. Amongst this collection was Huey P. Newton, George L Jackson, Jonathan Jackson, Bobby Seal, Fred Hampton and other members of The Black Panther Party. Bob Marley was also on his wall captured playing his guitar to one of his hit songs, "Buffalo Soldiers". Tupac was posted closest to the door.

Thang exited the bathroom to enter his room only to notice the music has been turned down. While staring in the mirror, he thought about what he said to his mom earlier. He didn't mean to hurt his mom, but every time he thinks about his coward of a dad, he lashes out without thinking. He also started to reminisce about his 18th birthday when he and Twurk were released from juvie. He couldn't wait to see his dad and had hopes that they all would turn up and visit the strip clubs together. Twurk agreed that it would be something fun to do with their father and then he pointed towards his mom coming in the Camry to pick the two of them up. She pulled into the parking area and hurried out of the car. She ran towards the twins with tears of joy in her eyes.

"Oh! My God! I'm so glad this day has finally come and my boys are free! Look at you two! You look just like your ...," she said failing to complete the sentence. She just stopped and stared at the two of them. "Who mom? We both look like who?" asked Thang. He had been excited to be able to show his dad all they had learned and how they have evolved into young men. The sad look on his mom's face and tears running down her face said it all. His happy mood had suddenly changed as his face and mouth tightened. His eyes were now a menacing squint and his fists now balled up like he was ready to hit someone.

Twurk felt the tension and rage rising up inside Thang, so he grabbed him and held him tightly. Their mom just fell to her knees and cried, "Baby! No!" Thang was quickly brought back to the present. He started to vibe along to the song over the speakers by DMX. "Thang's gon' give it to ya!" he rapped as he got dressed. Thang then stepped out of his room and realized that Twurk had just done the same. The two stared each other up and down as if they were about to set it off in the hallway. They both clapped their hands and silenced their music, then smirked at each other. They both gave a slight nod of the head indicating a mutual understanding.

Thang stepped up in Twurk's face. "Listen bruh, don't you ever threaten me again because it may get ugly next time!"
"Remember that can go either way. So, bring your A-game when you decide to bring it!" said Twurk with is smooth and cool counter attack.
"It will be more like my A+ game!" said Thang as he laughed along with Twurk. Twurk stopped laughing to give him a serious look. He said, "Bro, on the real though, Mom is all that we have left, so we gotta—". Before he could get out the next word, Thang cut him off. "I know bra, you done hit me with that same line about a million times!" he said. "Yeah, but you're acting as if you haven't learned anything from our builds." He saw that Thang was about to apologize so he said, "You owe me no apology.

Mom needs to know all that, not me!" said Twurk as he pointed in their mother's direction.

"I hate it when you're right!" said Thang staring at Twurk. He breathed in then exhaled before he made his way to find his mom. At this time, mom was on the porch staring out in to the evening clear sky except for the few blackbirds and an overhead plane going by as mother nature eased away her earlier tension. "So I guess your bro sent you out here to apologize, huh?" she said. Thang looked on in confusion and amazement because she was right." "What? What did you say? How did you know I was out here?" he asked. "You heard me!" she told him. "A mother knows her children, always!" she said staring in Thang's eyes. He can see the hurt on her face.

"Mom, I apologize for my rude behavior earlier. I wasn't thinking clear. You know how it can be sometimes, early in the morning and still half asleep. I can't take back what I said, but I do apologize and ask for your forgiveness." For the first time in a while, Thang realized how beautiful his mom was as he stared at her emerald green eyes that were wet with tears. He could see and feel her genuine love. "Yea, Thang, I do understand, but at the same time I try to be mindful and considerate, especially when it's a close and dear loved one," she reiterated. "Mom, you and Twurk are so much alike, kind of like the eye of the storm. I'm more like hurricane Hugo and can't wait to wreak havoc. Why am I like that mom? I need answers and I need them fast!" he said now feeling the depths of his mom's love and care for him.

"Son, not I nor Twurk can tell you anything for you will have to take the time and truly ask God to help you search your soul to find the answers to your true self. It is only then will you not continue being the same ole Thang, not knowing who you truly are and why you continue to hurt people. You two are all I have left. That's why I'm so concerned and protective over you. God forbid anything happen to you or your brother, I wouldn't have any reason to live. You two mean the world to me! I've been given a handsome, loving, strong and caring husband and now I have two grown men that look just like him. I thank God for that!" The two then embraced each other and smiled.

Inside Twurk answered the phone. "What's happenin' playa?" "Dis Red!" said the voice on the other end. Y'all two up for some B-ball?" "You know we are!" said Twurk. "The usuals are going to be there or are you going to scout for more talent?" said Twurk flexin' his confidence in his skills. "Man, you ain't all that! I think you done got rusty!" replied Red. "Red, you're absolutely right! I ain't all that, I'm all that and more!" said Twurk with a big smile across his face.

Moments later, mom & Thang came into the living room and saw Twurk moving about in the kitchen with quickness. "Dang! He's cooking breakfast again." They turned and looked at one another as they entered the kitchen giving each other a smirk as they shared an inside joke. "Two minutes and everything will be done," said Twurk who was moving around like kitchen like a chef. "Boy you know you got all my cooking skills!" said mom admiring Twurk's meal. "Yeah! All you're missing is the apron!" said Thang causing mom to erupt in laughter. He also joined in on the fun. "So, you two find this to be funny? I obviously missed the joke," said Twurk with a serious face. Mom and Thang got quiet, as the two exchanged looks.

Twurk bursted out laughing. "Now that was very funny! You two should have seen the hlooks on y'all's faces." Twurk stared at them laughing endlessly. Mom told him he had a great poker face because she thought he was serious. She asked if he needed any help with breakfast to which he replied, "No! I can handle it! You two just continue enjoying your little inside joke," he said with a bit of seriousness in his voice. "Oh Twurk, my baby, don't be like that! You know we're just playing!" said mom. "Yeah bruh! We're just having fun. Don't go getting all emotional on us," said Thang who clearly found the conversation humorous.

Twurk was quick to respond, but he stopped mid-sentence. They laughed again because they thought he got stuck on a word but actually his phone started vibrating then ringing. All that could be heard was "What it do playa? What yo side of the town be like?" The lyrics to Chances which was one of their favorite songs. They watched as mom bobbed her head along. Twurk answered the phone. "Dis Five! We throwing a special guest premiere party, then an exclusive after party. So, are you two down for tonight? Cause if one ain't down, then I know the other one ain't neither." Five was running his smooth lines to get them to commit.

"Let me check with Thang and I will get back at you. One!" With that, Twurk gave Thang a head nod that let him know what's up. Twurk served mom, Thang and himself a 5-star breakfast. After seeing the pleased looks of approval they all joined hands in prayer.

Afterwards they begin their own various conversations but ultimately ended up on the same page. "What is it, Twurk? Why are you all in my mouth and plate?" mom asked him. "Be honest with me mom!" Twurk replied. "Can I cook or what?" he asked. "What you trying to get cook of the year or something?" said Thang in a joking manner. "Ouch! What was that for?" snapped Thang. He had received a pinch from mom for teasing his brother. "Yes, son, you can cook just fine!" said Mom giving Twurk his props. "Thanks, mom! I try to do my best but I know I'll never outshine the master!" he said as he smiled as his mom. He turned to Thang and told him about the phone call he got from Red about playing some b-ball.

"Heck yeah! I'm always down for some b-ball!" said Thang with excitement. "Five hit me up too. He is having some kind of exclusive party and an after party, Twurk added. "That's right up my alley. We are definitely on for tonight!" said Thang. "So, I take it that you two will be out late tonight?" said mom to her sons. "Probably not, but we'll call in if we do," said Thang trying to charm his mom. "Promise me that you two will be safe!" said mom showing concern. "We promise we will be safe mom!" said Twurk and Thang in unison. Twurk's phone rang. "Damn! Y'all coming or what?" said Red on the other end. "It's packed and jumping out here!" Twurk and Thang looked at each other. "Don't worry about this little mess. The least I can do is clean up after you made me such a great meal," said mom.

"That's so nice of you, mom!" Thang kissed mom on the cheek then left the kitchen to get dressed up to play ball. Twurk told Red "Give us half an hour and we'll be there. You just make sure your money is on us. If not, it's lights out! Aight!" With that Twurk left to go get dressed. Mom stayed behind to clean up the mess. She didn't mind as she was happy to just have them home after 5 years of them being locked away.

"Damn! Why are you taking so long? You ain't doing nothing but changing!" said Thang. "Man, who the fuck you think you're rushing?" Twurk replied. Then they began to stare each other down. "Just like in high school!" said Twurk. "Yeah, but now we're better and older," replied Thang.

Twurk and Thang both kissed mom on their way out the door. They marveled over their Lincoln Navigator as they stepped outside. Cocaine white top with the words "The Inseparables" written on it, candy apple red bottom, 24-inch rims, and to top it all off, a booming system that you can hear almost a mile away. Twurk texted Five and told them they would be there tonight. Thang told Twurk that Five's girl, "Faith" had been trying to get with him on the low. "Have you told Five?" asked Twurk. "Hell no! That'll kill Five! You know how much he loves that girl. I wanted to, but when I see how happy he is with her, I just can't do it!" "Bro, you just have to follow your heart!" Twurk said. "I wish it was that easy. Maybe one day she'll slip up and Five will catch her red-handed," said Thang as he went into deep thought. What he didn't let Twurk know was that he had already hooked up with Faith and he was thinking of their time together and the many positions he had her in.

"Thang!" shouted Twurk. "Where did you go to that quick? One minute you're talking about Five & Faith, then you drifted off. I know you're trying to decide what you should do but time will let you know. Trust and believe that!" said Twurk. "Bro, you always seem to have all the right answers at the right times," said Thang. "Two heads are better than one!" said Twurk. They both laughed as this was a statement Twurk often repeated. They finally pulled into 'Hustler's', found them a spot to park, and scoped out the action-packed court. Before they hit the court Twurk had to roll up a blunt for them to smoke and put them in just the right mood to play. Thang started to cough and beat on his chest. "Damn! Where did they grow this at? Who did it come from?" he asked. "This shit is strong as fuck!"

"This some other shit, bro. I copped this from the omegas," said Twurk. He soon spotted Red walking towards their ride. They just continued to smoke and relax while listening to music.

Chapter 2

Red tapped on the window. They rolled down the window slowly. "What y'all two doing?" he asked. Twurk exhaled smoke in Red's face with a single raised eyebrow making sure Red got the message loud and clear. To which Red laughed and replied, "I understand y'all think y'all are some kind of celebs or something. We do have next! I don't know who they are, but they're from NY and they've been ballin' out there!" Red knew just how to get Twurk and Thang all fired up.

Twurk passed the blunt to Thang, then blew out a stream of smoke and looked into Red's eyes. "Well, let's see if we can put a stop to that!" said Twurk. They both got out of the ride. "Damn! I feel like I'm on top of the world!" said Twurk feeling himself. "Word! I feel the same way too! Let's go and serve these out-of-towners and show them how we country boys get down. It's showtime!" Thang said as he looked at the courts. Twurk then passed Thang the blunt as if he was passing the torch to get his teammate ready to roll. "You damn right! Let's go serve these city-slickers! We run these courts!", said Twurk.

Twurk took a pull from the blunt and locked the doors to the ride. They proceeded towards the basketball court with Red leading the way. It was on and they had money riding on this game as usual. Twurk & Thang were set to face off against the city slickers known as the "New York Ballers". From the time tip off occurred, they began to dominate the court. Twurk handled the ball like a pro. He shook his opponent with ease and handed the ball to Thang with a no-look pass. Thang dunked it with one hand which made the crowd go wild. The boys were always tight on defense, which is how they got the ball back to score again and again with two three pointers ending the game with 7-0 final score. They skunked the other team.

After the game, they were congratulated by the N.Y. Ballers as well as the crowd. They were crowned "King of Hustlers" for winning the game. They made sure to collect their winnings as well as the money for the bets they put down on themselves.

They were just that confident that they would come away with the win. Twurk & Thang both looked at Red because they knew he had bet against them. Twurk gave a wink and they both gave a big koolaid smile then walked away.

"Bro, we are the fucking best! You saw how the crowd started praising us and even the N.Y. Ballers had to recognize our skills! I know old Red felt like a real loser. He thinks we didn't know he betted against us" said Thang as he dapped up Twurk. They both had a good laugh as they made their way to their ride.

Twurk hit the security button and opened the door to the Navi. After removing his tank top, he then rolled up a victory blunt so he and Thang could smoke. After blowing smoke out the window of the ride, it was then he noticed a group of four chicks watching their every move. They were all thick just like he liked them, but one in particular caught his eye. She was about 5'5, 130 lbs pecan tan with long silky black hair. Her breasts were about a perfect C that highlighted her flat stomach with a belly ring. On her shirt was the symbol of a peach, which was fitting, because to Twurk she looked oh-so-juicy. She had some mesmerizing light green eyes that seem to pierce all the way through to the back of Twurk's mind. The type that you wouldn't just easily forget.

This sexy young chick that caught his eye went by the name of "Peaches". She was a part of Pink's crew. Pink, the ringleader, Peaches, Strawberry and Choc were all as thick as thieves and have ran the streets together since they were teens. She found herself also staring back at Twurk. In her mind, she wondered if he was single, how his body felt, what his sex game was like, and then she quickly snapped herself back into reality because she was staring way too long for her comfort and she's not the type to let a man throw her off her game. Her and her girls lived a lifestyle where there was no room for slippin', especially behind some man. But, looking at Twurk, she couldn't help the way she was feeling. Her girl, Strawberry, seeing the long drawn out trance her girl was in quickly diverted her eyes away from Twurk's.

Twurk still had his eyes on Peaches but later turned to look at his brother Thang. "Bro, do you see them four chicks over there looking at us?" said Thang not knowing that Twurk was already looking in their direction. "They all fine, but the chick with the strawberry streak in her hair and the strawberry symbol right on her coochie. I bet she got some blazing ass pussy!" said Thang as he licked his lips. "Bro, every woman with a pussy gots to have some good-good to you!" said Twurk with a laugh.

"So, you're saying chick with the strawberry don't got it going on?" asked Thang as he took a puff on the blunt. "She alright, but she ain't my type!" said Twurk. "Oh! I get it! I'm willing to bet you any amount of money that the girl with the peach on her shirt is your type," said Thang. "Maybe, and maybe not! Only time will tell, bro!", said Twurk. That was his way of attempting to get Thang to really think, especially when it comes to women. "Man, you always have to hit me with the philosophy! I respect it though! You do keep me on point, bro!" Thang realized.

Twurk became quiet and distant all of a sudden. "Twurk!" shouted Thang. "Dang bro! Where did you go that damn quick? You must be high as fuck or stuck on that chick!" Thang said as he laughed at his brother. "My bad, bro, if I seem distant. I've been thinking about a lot of different things lately. That's all, bro!" He had a lot of things on his mind but one of them was definitely, Peaches, the chick with the peach on her shirt. He contemplated as he took a pull off the blunt. Big Pun's "Still Not a Player' came on the stereo. Twurk slowly nodded his head to the song and he was especially feeling the hook as he thought about the chick he saw earlier.

"Damn! That chick had the most beautiful and sexiest eyes I've ever seen!" he thought to himself. Her eyes were telling me so much more, but what exactly, I can't quite put my hands on it yet. Man! I gotta shake this chick off my mind! It's not my style to be sweating or constantly thinking about some broad that I don't even know. These broads will set you up real quick!"

"Hey bro, I know you can feel this joint!" said Thang as he puts on Mobb Deep's song, "Get Away" and takes a pull on the blunt. "Bro, if anybody knows me, it's most definitely you!" said Twurk having a genuine moment with Thang as they pull into their driveway. "Tell me you two won?!" exclaimed mom as she met them coming through the door. "You already know that! We are born winners and survivors!" said Thang all amped up. "Well y'all winners need showers!" said mom. "Are y'all hungry?" said mom as she watched her sons walk off to their rooms. Thang went to his room thinking about the chick with the strawberry over the part he wanted the most. Twurk entered his room with thoughts going back to him and Thang back at juvie. He remembered when he got into his first fight while being incarcerated.

There was this big, burly Paul Bunyan looking C.O. who always gave them a hard time. One time in particular they were getting food and there was a beautiful lady serving the chicken that day. She smiled at Twurk and gave him two pieces of chicken on his tray. That day, one of the other inmates by the name of P-Murder, who kind of ran the joint was also in the line. He had the look of Rick Ross but with a Booker T build. He was the resident "boss". Every move or call had to be run by him first. This day he was peeping Twurk and Thang out from afar. He noticed Twurk getting two pieces of chicken and decided to approach them when they got to their table.

"Hey green eyes! That bird is mines! She just placed it on the wrong tray. Maybe she got lost in those colorful eyes of yours," said P-Murder as he chuckled deeply. "I don't think she did. Especially, when she looked me in the eyes before she placed it on my tray and not yours. So, whatever you're talking about, I ain't trying to hear it!" said Twurk.

"Fuck you!" shouted P-Murder as he swung on Twurk knocking him off the stool. Thang immediately jumped up, but before he could get at P-Murder, he was overtaken by four dudes who placed a beatdown on him. P-Murder and three other dudes were pounding out Twurk as the crowd in the café starting yelling "fight!" "fight!" "fight!". Twurk remembered P-Murder as

14

he stood over him telling him as he did earlier, "I told you she placed that chicken on your tray for me! And by the way, look at how you're making that bitch cry! You two are my bitches now, so welcome to my world!" P-Murder left with Twurk & Thang's three pieces of chicken and his entourage laughing along the way.

Twurk crawled over to Thang then looked at all the individuals jumping up and down while screaming as the C.O.'s tried to apprehend them. The lady who placed the two chickens on his tray stood staring at Twurk and Thang with tears in her eyes and her hand over her mouth. Twurk looked down at Thang and said, "I promise you on my life, we will not slip like this ever again or let anyone hurt you or me again while we are back here! We will get them all back in due time. I promise you that!" He had passed out afterwards and thus ended the flashback snapping Twurk back into the present. He proceeded to go take a shower.

Thang went into the living room to find his mom's eyes glued to the TV. "Jerry! Jerry! Jerry!" were the sounds coming across the room. "Hey mom!" said Thang loudly, knowing he would catch his mom off guard. "Boy! Don't you ever sneak upon me like that again! You gon' mess around and give me a heart attack!" said mom clutching her chest while squinting her eyes at him.

"You shoulda saw the look on your face!" said Thang as he laughed uncontrollably. "What you two got going on?" said Twurk as he entered the room. "Just your damn brother trying to give me a heart attack. Sneaking up on me like that while I'm trying to watch my Jerry Springer show," said mom as she went to get their plates from the kitchen. "I understand you two will be out tonight, but I will like to know where you will be?" said mom with a concerned straight face. "We're going to a party at Five's club, then an afterparty next," said Thang.

Suddenly, the the phone rang. "What's happenin' playa?" answered Twurk. "Man, I need you and Thang to bring me a few cases of blunts. I was so busy and tied up that I couldn't get out to grab any for the party," said Five on the other end. "No doubt!" said Twurk. "Thanks!" said Five as he ended the call. After they finished their food, they both gave their mom a hug and a kiss before they left the house.

They pulled up to the store and Twurk got out the ride. He asked Thang if he needed anything from inside before he shut the door. The first thing on his mind was some OJ because the weed he smoked earlier gave him cottonmouth. He proceeded to go down the aisle where he bumped into someone he knew from the past by the name of Diamond. "Oh my God! Twurk is that really you? I can't believe this! It has been so long since I've seen you. Damn! You look so fucking good and sexy too! Where did you disappear to and why wasn't I informed?" she said. He stared at her for a minute admiring her black hair and grey eyes. She resembled Rosie Perez but was a black Dominican.

"Good to see you too!" he said with the smile of a Cheshire cat. "I see you are still as beautiful as the last time I saw you. Also, I see you done got married. So, who's the lucky man?" he said admiring her ring. She stared back at him but at a loss for words at the moment. Meanwhile outside, Thang was outside vibing to the music blasting through the speakers when Pink and her crew pulled up to the store. Pink exited her money green Lexxus that was sitting on 22-inch rims. She glanced at the Navi before entering the store so she knew there was a chance Twurk might be inside.

Thang watched as the women walked in the store. He started daydreaming about sexing Strawberry. While inside the store, Twurk grabbed a 6 pack of orange juice. Then, he walked with Diamond down the aisle towards the counter. Memories of he and Diamond came flooding back through his mind all at once. Diamond, was not feeling the silence and awkward tension between the two of them. She wanted to come right out and tell Twurk how she feels, but afraid of how he will respond, she keeps it to herself. She watched as Twurk asked for a case of blunts and proceeded to pay for all his items including her pack of Juicy fruit chewing gum and Coke. They both turned to leave the store.

Peaches saw Twurk and Diamond leaving the store. She shook her head as she missed the chance to catch up with him. "Looks like somebody is having a party! Too bad, I'm attending one tonight myself cause I would have loved to follow his fine sexy ass!" she said to herself with a smile.

Once outside, Twurk dropped his items off to his ride and walked Diamond to her vehicle. "Diamond, you still haven't told me who's the lucky man," he insisted. "Twurk, when you disappeared, I just didn't know what to do. I met this Italian guy who swept me off my feet but he also just happens to be one of the biggest drug lords around. We ended up getting married. I hope you're not mad at me?" said Diamond with tears in the corner of her eyes. This made her look even more sexy and beautiful to Twurk. Once they got to her car, which was a shiny red Jag, Twurk even opened the door for her. He felt her soft hand touch his, as they locked eyes standing just inches apart. "Twurk, I miss you so much! What happened to us, baby? We used to be.." she stopped suddenly and started to shake her head slowly. She started thinking back on the time they spent together.

"I know and I do miss you too, Diamond, but if you don't change then we will always be cool and have each other's hearts, but that's it," he finished. "Twurk, I still love you!" said Diamond as she leaned in to Twurk to kiss him passionately. She stepped back while biting her lip and slowly got inside car. Twurk, still the gentlemen, closed her door and watched as Diamond pulled off. Twurk basked in the moment for a minute then turned to go get in his ride. "Damn! Who the fuck was that chick?" asked Thang as he rolled up a blunt. "That was Diamond. You know the chick I was fucking with before---" "Yeah! I remember now! How did you fuck up with her?" said Thang cutting off Twurk.

"Bro, you already know how the game go! We don't love them hoes!" said Twurk giving Thang a high-five although deep down inside it wasn't true. They pulled off to head to the party.

"Girl, did you see that? He's rolling around with this chick pushing a Jag. His sex game must be off the hook!" said Pink. "Or that nigga must have some major bread!" her girl Choc piped in. "A mark!" they both said in unison. Peaches was thinking differently. She had fallen for Twurk a little harder than she would like to admit to herself and to her girls.

"Peaches, I know you was checking out that twin and that chick he was with! I think we should pay more close attention to them twins and that chick. We may strike and come across something worth the effort," Strawberry said to Peaches as she passed her a Smirnoff.

"Who the fuck was driving that money green Lexus?" Twurk asked Thang. "You remember them four chicks at the park? I saw that strawberry coochie chick get out of the Lexus. I know you saw her in the store!" said Thang with a smirk on his face while he reclined in the seat. "Yea I saw them!" said Twurk. "I know one thing though, if them chicks think we are a sweet lick, then they all will be in a for a bad day and a long rest. They continued to make their way to the club.

Chapter 3

"Y'all niggaz gonna make me kill one of y'all! Or better yet, all of y'all!" shouted P-murder. "I sent y'all to do something simple. Fuck-ups is all the results I'm getting!" he continued letting his crew have it. "Shit happens like that when you send boys to do a man's job" added Roc, who reminded most of a light skinned version of the rapper Young Buck from G-Unit.

"So what are you implying, Roc? That we can't handle business? Cause the last time I checked, we 'pose to be a team. No big I's or little u's. What happened to that?", Heat barked back in response. He was a medium build and resembled the rapper, Freeway in his Roc-a-fella days.

"Y'all two just need to get that shit off y'all chest!" said Reaper, interjecting in his two cents. He was the straight shooter of the crew. "I know where them four chicks are gonna be tonight!" Jitty the comedian of the crew piped in. "You talking about Pink and her crew?" asked P-Murder making sure he heard Jitty correctly.

"I sure am man! I heard from a reliable source that they are gonna be at "Playas & Ballers" tonight. I even heard two new artists are also performing their tonight, but no names though. Jitty was all smiles by now. "Well, well, well, Jitty has saved the day. Y'all should be thanking him. He did bail y'all out. Ain't that right, Roc?" said P-murder as he looked over all the surrounding faces that were staring back at him and ultimately locked eyes with Roc who wasn't feeling it.

"So what Jitty found out some valuable information! Who's to say they won't fuck up again?" Roc barked back as he didn't like being put on the spot since he is P-murder's first in command. "Don't hate the playa, hate the game!" replied Jitty now with a serious face. "If you got something to get off your chest, go ahead! Your words ain't nothing but an invitation to an ass-whooping!" he continued.

"Y'all two, calm down! Save your energy and anger for our four special girls. Tonight, we will be attending "Playas & Ballers"! Live and in full effect! So, do anyone here oppose, or are y'all with me?" he said in a loud voice. They all agreed in unison. P-Murder glanced around at all the loyal, ready-to-body-anybody soldiers he had in his presence. They soon were on their way.

They arrived at the club just in time to hear the last parts of a song performed by a group called "Fiah" which had the crowd going wild. Five, the emcee for the night, asked the crowd to give it up for the group one more time which leads to a rush of applause and chants. P-Murder and his crew made their way through the rowdy crowd to find a spot on the back wall where they can post up as they scope through the crowd.

As the next group took the stage to perform their song, in walks Pink and her crew. They made their way to the first available table. They immediately started getting into the groove. After the group's set is over, Five, made his way to the stage to announce the next group but he is nervously looking at his watch because he is thinking Twurk and Thang may not show up on time. "Alright, Twurk & Thang, I really need y'all to show up!" he thought to himself. Little did he know that they had just pulled up to the club just as he brought out the next act. To avoid the crowd, they knew would be hyped up already, they decided to use the secret entrance to the club. When Five saw them, he nearly choked on his words. He left to the stage to make sure everything was ready to go for the next set which would feature Twurk and Thang.

Meanwhile, at the table occupied by the most wanted four girl posse, Pink has been noticing the distant stare in her girl's eyes. She proposed a toast. "To a happy & never- ending friendship!" "Right Peaches?" she added. They all turned to look at her. "What you say, Peaches?" asked Pink trying to get her girl's attention. She looked at them suddenly and realized they must have caught her daydreaming. "Of course! Forever!" They all took a sip of Moet! At the back of the club posted on the wall P-Murder and his boys could be seen taking a puff of blunts and drinking. All eyes from the crowd suddenly turned to the stage as Five made his way to the mic. "Welcome to the stage, Twurk and Thang!"

The crowd grew quiet as the lights went dim and then turned red. Special effects made it appear as if red rain was falling on everyone. Twurk and Thang hit the stage wearing matching gear. They both donned a diamond earring in their right ear that blinded the audience when the light hit it just right. They wore no shirts to show off their tattoos and athletic physiques, a scorpion chain with their names spelled out in small red diamonds on the tail and to complete the attire, red jeans with a fresh pair of red J's. They looked like every woman's dream and the man other men loved to hate. They began to give the audience a show worth their money.

Five stared out at them from the VIP's skybox window as he sipped from his glass of champagne. He was admiring the creativity of the set that Twurk & Thang had put together. "Tonight is going to bring in a lot of money!" he thought. "I know ole boy should've called me back by now! I just got that gut-feeling that those two down there are gonna make it big one day! Who the fuck they think they are anyway? Prince or somebody?" he continued as he laughed to himself.

The audience was vibin' and singing along to the hook of Twurk & Thang's song, "Chances". Back in P-Murder's crew, Roc was not too thrilled. "Fuck them niggas!" he said to himself. Reaper, Jitty and Heat made their way to the bar. As Thang belted out, "They say hell is hot and heaven is the cool spot. I'm so close to glory so why you tryna end my story!" it suddenly clicked to P-Murder why they seemed so familiar. He flashed back to his time in juvie. "That's where I know them from!" he said to himself. "You and your twin are so right and so dead!" he continued giving a menacing stare in their direction.

Peaches was so into the song as she began to think about how she saw Twurk was kissing on the chick back at the store. However, despite his dealings with another chick, she still has a deep desire for him. She hears Twurk rapping the words, "I ain't never scared, shawty let's take a chance!" and she felt he was singing it only to her.

Five was loving the interaction and feedback from the crowd for Twurk & Thang. He's used to them freestyling over raw hand-made beats and beatboxing but adding in the special effects just took them to another level. In came Red, late as usual. "My bad man!" he started. "You know I got into it with my ole lady! Talking about I spend too much time down at the courts and not enough time with her". "Again?" said Five, a little less surprised because this wasn't the first or second time. To change the subject and end the saga that was about to be spilled, he told Red to pour himself a drink and check out Twurk and Thang on the stage.

"Yo! Ain't that Pink and the crew? Look over there at the girls chilling at the table!" said Jitty to Heat & Reaper. Heat and Reaper were starting to get amped up while looking around to find them. They were ready to blaze anyone at any minute. "Over there you two fools! And stop looking so damn obvious!" said Jitty, keeping a cool head. "Yea! That's them fine ass bitches! I want to fuck them real good before we kill their treacherous asses," said Reaper. "Man you're sick!" Heat told Reaper. They went to find P-Murder to tell him the news. "Pink and her crew are here, just as I told you they would be," Jitty told P-Murder as he passed him a bottle of Bacardi Black. He then turned to look at Roc who was receiving a bottle from Reaper. He could see the irritation written all over his face.

Twurk & Thang were still on stage as moved into another song in their set called the "Magic Man". The beat and the lyrics coupled with the appeal of the twins had the ladies in the crowd going wild. So much so that the bouncers had to come stand in front of the stage. As they belt out their verses to the crowd, the ladies seem to almost overpower the guards trying to make their way to the stage. Twurk pulled Thang back a little because he peeped what was going on. Five, peeped it too so he started to prep their stage exit. He then hit the switch, the lights went out and then suddenly back on. Twurk and Thang had disappeared (like magic men).

"Damn! Those twins were fucking fire!" said Jitty all hyped up. Reaper and Heat were watching the women that were going wild over them. Roc looked on with a devilish grin and blew out a puff of smoke from his nostrils. "Run! Run! Run as fast you can gingerbread twins! Y'all days are numbered!" thought P-Murder to himself as he was scoping out Pink and her crew.

"Alright, ladies and gentlemen, I hope---I mean, I know," he said while laughing, "y'all were definitely feeling my boys Twurk & Thang. The crowd got hype as they showed love for the twins. "That was just a sample and taste of what's to come. If you like what you just saw you can follow them on Facebook and Twitter. Log on to their website, twurkandthangtheinseparable.com to hear more of what they have to offer. Most importantly go to our Five's Up & Coming Stars page on Facebook and vote on who you think the next local star should be. With that said, let's get ready for the aftershow," said Five, ready to get the party jumping.

Strawberry and Choc both made their way to the dance floor as Sisqo's "Thong song" started playing. They both were approached by dudes that looked like ballers so they were beyond ready to dance up on them. Pink turned to Peaches and said, "You know the drill! Let's go get paid, honey!" and she grabbed Peaches by the hand to go to the dance floor. Roc and Heat approached Pink and Peaches to dance as soon as they hit the floor. They agreed to their requests, not knowing the danger that was close by.

"Man! That was a close call! Them shawties be going crazy!" Twurk told Thang. "We smashed that performance! It feels so good to be on top!" Thang said in reply as he took a seat in the VIP room to roll a blunt. "Yeah, we are the best!" Twurk adds as he looked through the skybox window down at the crowd. For some reason, he still was thinking of Peaches, whom he saw at the court earlier. He almost lost his mind when he saw the same girl out on the dance floor dancing with some dude. Peaches was on the floor grinding up on Heat but she definitely had Twurk on the brain and wishes it were him she was dancing with as the words from his song played over and over in her brain.

"Man, you ok?" asked Thang as he noticed how quiet and distant Twurk suddenly became.

On the dance floor, Pink and her crew were exchanging glances. Pink was also looking around and taking in the action going on inside the club as well as the many faces present. Even though she didn't readily see any known potential threats, she was too street smart not to know someone was watching. Peaches was in her own zone. The DJ played a slow song "Please Don't Judge Me" by Chris Brown. The lyrics seem to take her away and reaches the most sensitive parts of her soul. She still felt Twurk's presence even after seeing their disappearing act earlier. She felt his eyes on her in some way.

Up in the skybox, Thang walked over and stood beside Twurk to pass him the blunt as he too glanced out the window down at the crowd. He saw Strawberry on the floor along with her other girls dancing with dudes he was unfamiliar with. "Fucking tricks!" he thought to himself. "Bro, let's get out of this bitch. We already been here too long!" he told Twurk. "Yea, bro you are right! Ain't like there's much to do up in here," Twurk replied.

Later on outside the club, Strawberry and Choc exchanged numbers with the "ballers" they were dancing with on the dance floor. So, Pink then turns to Roc and ask for his number. "Nah, let me get your number!" he said in return. After eyeing Roc, she gave in and gave him her number. "You better call me!" she said to him. Heat is now feeling confident and asks for Peaches' number. "I guess I can! You did behave yourself," said Peaches as she gave Heat her number.

Pink and her crew made their way to their ride and pulled off with Ciara's "My Goodies" blasting through the windows as if to send a subtle message. Roc and Heat gave each other dap, as the rest of their crew came out to join them. They all got into the

Hummer and pulled off with the music blasting. "Push it to the limit!" yelled Heat from the rear passenger window.

"Yo P-Murder, those bitches are gonna be easy man!" Roc told P-Murder. "That's what I'm talking about!" P-Murder replied. "I don't know man. That bitch I was with....Don't get me wrong or nothing, but she just seemed so different but also a little distant. I just can't put my finger on it quite yet," said Heat. "Yeah! Just like your dick too. Ain't it?!" teased Jitty and Reaper causing everyone to laugh but Heat. "Aight! Aight! We did good tonight. I'm proud of everyone for playing their positions. Now all we have to do is wait for the flies to land in the web. Then BAM! We crush them!" said P-Murder to his crew. He thought to himself, "Pink was looking real good tonight! Before this is all over, I'm going to see for myself just how good she really is."

As Twurk and Thang were headed home, Thang noticed his brother with a somber look and he tried to lighten the mood a bit. "Bro, why you so damn quiet for? It's like you done lost your best friend or something?" Twurk glanced over at Thang and gave him a look that they both mutually understood. Thang gave Twurk the blunt, which helped relax his mind as he thought about what happened at "Playas & Ballers". He thought about how they smashed their live performance and how all the women were about to rush the stage and ambush them. It felt like they were real-life superstars. Then, he thought about the chick with the sexy green eyes from the basketball court and how she was dancing with that dude on the dance floor. At one moment, she looked up in his direction as he was looking at her although she didn't know he was there. It seemed as though she felt his presence. He was vibin' along with the music and deep in thought until Thang disrupted it to tell him to pass the blunt. All he could do was pass it and smile.

On the other side of town, Pink and her girls just arrived at their four-bedroom house. "I'll be inside, shortly. I need some time alone to myself," said Peaches to her girls, taking them by surprise. "Girl, what the fuck is wrong with her?" Strawberry asked Peaches. "C'mon y'all!" Let Peaches have her "privacy"!" said Choc to her girls as they went inside.

"Bro, I'm beat. I'm about to hit the shower and call it a night. You good, bruh?" said Thang to Twurk. "Yeah, I'm okay. I just had so much on my mind, that's all. I'm straight now though, bro!" said Twurk. "I'm gonna check in on mom before I call it a night," he added. They did their signature handshake and Twurk headed to the back. Thang took a quick peak in his mom's room before heading to the shower. After, taking a shower he headed straight to bed with Strawberry on his mind. He was still determined to get him a piece!

Twurk opened his mom's room door. The moonlight shining in on her through the window showed how peaceful she looked sleeping. The creaky sound on the door caused her to awaken. She then turned on her bedside lamp. "Twurk! That's you baby? What's wrong and where is Thang?" Y'all had me a little worried. Y'all didn't call me, but how did my babies do tonight?" said mom to Twurk.

"How did you know it was me and not Thang?" said Twurk. "It's called a mother's intuition. We have that naturally you know? Thang, he will come to the door to check on me, but he doesn't come all the way in. You two are like night and day, but I love you both unconditionally," she said. "Mom, you can go back to sleep. Just know that Thang and I rocked the place! We had women falling out and almost getting trampled over when they tried to rush the stage. Luckily, we made our "magic" getaway. Thang is fine. He should be in bed by now," said Twurk.

Twurk, what's wrong? It's written all over your face. Who's the young woman that has my baby so lost?" asked mom showing concern. "How do you know it's a female and not nothing else?" Twurk replied, not liking to be read so easily. "Son, I carried you and your brother for nine months. I know more than you two think I know. So, tell me what's bothering my baby and don't lie to me!" mom replied with a smile on her face. She sat up in the bed and pat a spot on the bed for Twurk to sit down.

"It's this shawty I saw after the ball-game. When I locked eyes with her, it was like love at first sight, sort of. As I told you earlier Thang and I killed the show at "Player and Ballers'. As the night started winding down we were chilling up in the sky box. Straight VIP! I guess it was by chance but I looked down on the dance floor and I saw her dancing with this dude. I felt like that dude was supposed to be me. When I looked into her beautiful eyes, I felt I saw my soul mate," said Twurk to his mom being as honest as he can about his most intimate feelings.

"Aww! Look at my baby! You finally done found you someone! And I take it that you don't know if it's for sure or not?" said mom as she weighed her options on what advice to give. "Son, just follow your heart. Next time you see her try to conversate with her because maybe she feels the same way about you. She may be struggling on how to come at you just like you're struggling," said mom as she stared into Twurk's eyes. She smiled appreciating the open communication in the relationship she shares with him. "Thanks, mom! I don't know how, but you always seem to have all the right answers at the right times. I hope when I do find Mrs. Right that our relationship will be in sync with one another's lives. Alright mom, go back to sleep. We'll talk some more tomorrow if it's God's will. I love you mom!" he added before planting a kiss on her forehead and turning to walk out the door. She then turned off the lamp and returned comfortably to her cozy sleep position in her bed as she muttered the words "Thank you God!" before closing her eyes.

After taking a quick shower, Twurk entered his room and started reflecting back on his mom's advice. He smiled at the facts of how throughout everything, mom had been both the woman and man of the house. He turned on his stereo just before his head hit the pillow. A love song played over the speaker, Sisqo's "Incomplete"

Chapter 4

Peaches walked over to the swing to sit down and started swinging back and forth slowly. She couldn't help but notice how good of a condition that the two-seater swing set was still in after all these years from when they first bought the house from this elderly couple. Her mind traveled back to the day she first met the girls. She was in a fight getting jumped by a bunch of girls. The leader of the pack had a face like the rapper Khia. She was getting the best of Peaches, punching her all in her neck and her back. Then she saw three more girls come running up and she thought she was about to get jumped. "Ahh! Y'all bitches trying to jump me? So, this is how it's going down, huh? I beat y'all bitch up and y'all coming to jump a real bitch! Fuck y'all!" Then all of a sudden, she saw two of the girls whom she later learned were named Strawberry and Choc start stumping the loud-mouthed girl she was fighting before they got there.

Peaches watched as this chick with pink hair come rolling up on the action with ease giving off a boss-like aura. She looked into Peaches' eyes and smiled briefly before extracting a shiny switchblade. She kneeled down then gave the chick who was now on the ground a "buck-fifty" across her left cheek. After everything had taken place, Peaches found herself hanging out with them afterwards and they kind of been thick as thieves ever since. She was quickly brought back to the present when she was bitten on her arm by a mosquito. She quickly went inside to find everyone else fast asleep. So she took a quick shower then dozed off as images of the guy from the basketball courts earlier that day invaded her mind.

At P-Murder's crib, he and his crew had just settled in from the club. "Roc, that chick you were with, what's she about?" P-Murder asked. "Its' hard to say, but I got this!" Roc flashed the piece of paper Pink gave him with her number on it. They dapped each other up with a little laughter. Jitty and Reaper entered the room, followed by Heat, who obviously has something important to say.

"Y'all won't believe this shit! That green eyed...! That bitch gave me a fake ass number!" he said as the crew laughed. "Nah! Check this out! That's not even the fucked-up part!"

"Oh shit! Let me get the popcorn!" Jitty interrupted trying to be comical to which Heat gave him an ice grill expression in return. "So, I called the number. The line went through. In my mind, I was like "Hell yeah! I got this bitch! Man! Some old lady answered the phone!" The crew erupted in laughter. "Hold up y'all! This is the fucked-up part. The old lady says" Billy! Billy! Billy is that you?" "Hell no! This ain't no mutha fuckin' Billy! Then she started chanting some damn prayer. Talkin' about I am the devil and need some holy cleansing! I just hung up the phone on that old bitch!" said Heat who was mad as hell but also had to laugh at the situation along with the crew. They gave Heat a hard time for the rest of the night.

In the morning, Peaches got up to make breakfast for the girls to show her appreciation. "Damn! You really put your foot in this food! Cause this shit is delicious, Peaches!" complimented Strawberry. "Yea! You can cook Peaches, but what I don't get is that last night you were acting all distant. It's like you were in a far-away land or something. Then you got up to cook this blazing ass breakfast and your mood is the total opposite. Girl, did you get you some dick last night or something?" Pink then glanced over at Strawberry and Choc. They all looked back at Peaches and started laughing.

"Girl, did y'all see that guy I was dancing with last night?" said Strawberry as they were discussing all that went down at Playas & Ballers. "What about that guy, huh?" interrupted Choc who was obviously feeling some type of way as she cut her eyes at Strawberry. She then stormed off from the table and out of the kitchen. "Well! Well! Ain't this great!" said Pink trying to break up the tension. She didn't like when they argued. "I better go check on her!" said Strawberry. "Peaches will you...?" she stopped mid-sentence as she passed Peaches her dish. Peaches knew exactly what she meant with both statements. "Just go! I will take care of the dishes!" she said as she playfully tried to stop Strawberry from giving her a kiss out of gratitude. "Girl, stop! I don't know where your lips been!" she laughed and Strawberry lightly pinched her on the arm.

Strawberry, after wrapping herself in nothing but a towel, made her way to the bathroom. She cracked open the shower door as was overtaken by the hot steam and sweet-smelling body wash along with Choc's chinky eyes penetrating her. She then let the towel drop to the floor and followed Choc's finger urging her to come into the shower. Peaches, who was in the middle of washing dishes, laughed to herself at how crazy in love Strawberry and Choc are with each other. "Those are my girls though!" she thought to herself.

Deciding to get an early start on the day, Thang is up and running when he hears the phone ring and answers it. "Yo bro, Five is on the line!" he screamed out to Twurk. He didn't hear a response, and decides to call out again. He hates calling out someone's name only to not get a response. He didn't get a response this time either so he figured he might still be asleep. "Hold on Five, He must still be sleep or something," said Thang. He then proceeded to walk towards Twurk's room. Twurk was in a deep sleep dreaming about his father. "Son, one thing I want you and your bro to always remember. You either the hunter or the hunted!" he said as he normally would when he dropped jewels of wisdom on them. Then the dream flipped to when Twurk & Thang got their rep and respect in juvie. P-Murder along with four other members of his juvie crew doing their routine locker checking. "Well, look at who done made it back down! Ain't them the same two we punished for that chicken? I also heard they making some major moves around here!" said P-Murder trying to rile up his crew.

Thang jumped up with the quickness. "Fuck y'all! Cause ain't shit sweet over here motherfucker! Let's get it!" he said. "I got 'em!" said Gunz, who came rushing at Thang, along with his cohort Pinz. Thang caught Gunz with a 2-piece and ducked in the nick of time to avoid a quick, wild swing from Pinz. Then caught him with an uppercut and a right to the chin that put him straight to sleep. Thang was amped up and bouncing from foot to foot looking at his work.

"Get him! I want them dead!" screamed P-Murder, now all pissed off. "We got 'em!" said Doom who was one of the bigger members of the crew. Moving right beside him was Shock who could easily pass for his twin, except Doom was dark skinned and Shock was an albino and a bit cockeyed. They both pulled out machetes made from lawn mower blades then they both charged at Twurk. P-Murder stood with a smirk on his face. Twurk cracked his neck to get himself loose, then gave Thang a wink. "Yo! Watch my work!" he told Thang. Doom took a wild swing that might have split Twurk into if he had not taken a quick side step. He quickly grabbed Doom's outer wrist and kicked him on the side of the knee to break his leg. Then he hit him with a 2 piece to the chin sending him to bed early. He took Doom's weapon and used it to bait Pinz who swung his machete in his direction. He met Pinz's machete mid-air with the machete he got from Doom and sent Pinz's machete flying through the air. Pinz's eyes followed the weapon. Twurk, then caught Pinz with a fast and stiff kick to the side of the face, which didn't break Pinz neck but he didn't come back conscious to an hour later. Twurk turnt in P-Murder's direction. He locked eyes with him and signaled for him to come get some too. Twurk was ready for action and was getting prepared to fight when Thang's shaking him caused him to wake up in a fighting stance.

"Hold on, Bruce Leroy! It's just me letting you know that Five is on the line. Damn! Who was after you? The devil?" said Thang as he left out of the room laughing at Twurk. "What's poppin', homie? Y'all fucking rocked the club last night! Boy, I put y'all out there! This site gets some big-time producers! I gotta show y'all this damn site. Yo! I'm having a cook-out today. Y'all gonna be able to attend? It's at 2:00!" added Five. "Shit! What did Thang say?" asked Twurk sleepily. "He said he's with it" replied Five. "I'll see y'all at 2!" Twurk ended the call.

Thang was outside by the Navi on the phone with one of his steady chicks named Lola. He messed around with a lot of women but he had real feelings for Lola even though he did her dirty sometimes. They'd go through stretches of time without seeing each other. During the last stretch, Lola got into the drug game due to her drug addicted brother and his debt along with her lust for the finer things something she would never tell Thang because he would not condone it nor forgive her for doing so. "What's up mami?" he said trying to be charming. "Ain't nothing papi! Just missing the fuck out of you!" she said in return. "When am I going to see you again? It's like you're avoiding me!" she continued. "Don't act like that! You know I am going to slide through later!" he said knowing that he is lying through his teeth. "Yeah, right!" said Lola who has heard it all before. With that, they ended the call. He started to reminisce on how they met. She bumped into him knocking his things out of his hands. She apologized right away and helped him pick up his stuff. He remembered being on the ground as she was bent over and all he could see was a red thong and the print of a fat kitty kat. Just the mere thought was getting him hard all over again. He thought to himself that he just might need to pay Lola a visit. Twurk interrupted Thang's moment back in time to tell him they needed to clean the ride. So, they headed to Pop's car wash.

Pink and the crew were at Pop's car wash, bright and early, putting on a show for all the passers-by. The car wash became packed so fast and they nearly caused a wreck with all their antics. Peaches, was having fun with her girls physically but mentally she was someplace else. With everything that her and her girls have been through together, she just doesn't feel the same rush anymore. She was feeling different about their lifestyle now. A splash of water from Strawberry brought her out of her trance. "Girl! What the fuck!" as she proceeded to get her right back, which just amped up the moment even more.

Twurk and Thang pulled into the same car wash 20 minutes after their show was over. They both got out followed by a trail of smoke lingering upwords. The owner of the business recognizes them and comes to greet them from behind the booth window. He couldn't wait to tell them what just went down. "Y'all two missed one of the world's greatest shows at the car wash ever! And I got it all on tape! Y'all want to see it, young bloods?" he asked all hyped up and glaring at them through his bifocals.

"No thanks!" they said in unison." "We do appreciate the thought though, but we just here to wash this truck and leave" Twurk added. Thang, who always found Pops to be very funny, laughed, and so did Twurk.

"I never in my whole life seen such fine and sexy women! Here I was thinking it was going to be an ordinary day. Then. Bam! Them four chicks came and turnt this motherfucker out! We almost had two wrecks here too!" Pops said, looking at Twurk and Thang. He was serious but all they could do was just laugh. "Pops, you should have been a comedian! You are so damn hilarious! You got me laughing so hard; my stomach hurts!" said Thang who laughed so hard and got choked from the laughter and the blunt so he passes it to Twurk. "I recognize that smell anywhere!" said Pops. "That...That..That's that damn loud pack, ain't it! Ain't that the word for it nowadays? That shit gotta be good. Making me stutter!" said Pops to Twurk thinking he was going to get something to smoke on like he's a youngin' in the game. "Man, anytime we got it, you got it. I ain't never laughed this much and this hard before!" said Thang as he gave Pops a bag of loud. "You need a dutch, Pops?" asked Thang as he held out a Dutch cigar.

"Hell no! Y'all go them 20th century lungs! Shit! I got old lungs! I keep it straight old school. Today was almost like my birthday! I saw half naked women, got some loud, and got my good ole buddy Jack Daniels waiting for me at the house! What that rapper with all them golds say?" asked Pops. "Oh! Yeah! Pop a molly and I'm sweating! Woo!" he answered. "Y'all thought ole Pops here ain't know about Trinidad James, huh? Shit! I can rap too! Smoke this loud and I'm coughing!" as he coughed and walked off. They burst out laughing as they finished cleaning the ride to head to the cook out.

"Red! What are you doing, man? You must be burning the fuck out of them steaks!" said Five. "Look there go our boys!" he added. "What's poppin, Five? What y'all got going on out here?" asked Twurk as he and Thang dapped Five up.

"That damn Red! He know he can't drink and cook! Surprised his hair ain't caught on fire yet with all them damn chemicals in it!" said Five to Twurk and Thang. They all started laughing along with Red who raised his glass to them but kept on cooking and dancing to Rick James' "Mary Jane". They start to discuss Five's upcoming bachelor party and they tease him about being "locked down" and having a "warden". "Hey y'all hungry asses! The food is ready! Come get it!" said Red who by now is tipsy to say the least. They all rushed the grill at once.

P-Murder and his crew were kicking up dust in the streets on the Spanish side of town. They were holding hostages and intending to collect what was owed. "Bitch ass nigga!" said Roc as he pistol-whipped the male who was visibly doped up. The woman screamed at him to stop so he kicked her in the face sending her to the floor with a bloody mouth and nose. "Shut up bitch!" he added. P-Murder stood over Lola's badly bruised body as Heat, Jitty and Reaper at roughed her up prior. "Lola, you was my main chick when it came to the hustle game, Then, you went and let this dope head come and fuck with my money! It's not personal though, it's just business!" said P-Murder as he nodded to Roc who then placed two shots to the guy's head. P-Murder then shot the woman before she could let out a scream. Afterwards, they all got into the Hummer and pulled with the music blasting like nothing happened. They were on to the next move.

Their next mark was some Haitian kid known as Money, that was well known around the block for stacking major dough. He was on the court playing ball with his boys, Pile- Up, who was his right-hand man, plus Grilz and Juice, who made up the rest of his running crew. After the game, Money and Pile-Up took off leaving Grilz and Juice behind. P-Murder told Roc and Heat to take care of them but leave them alive. As Grilz and Juice start to throw the ball around when they see two unfamiliar faces come rolling up. "Yo! Let me holla at y'all for a second! Y'all are them up top ballers, right?" said Roc trying to lure them. Juice looked at Grilz then back at the men approaching. Juice suddenly threw the ball at Roc's head and then they both took off running. "Fuck! Y'all motherfuckers are dead!" said Roc now highly pissed off. He and Heat took off after them.

P-Murder watching from afar, sees the action that's transpiring so he gunned the Hummer. They were so focused on getting away they didn't see the Hummer coming. They were blindsided like a quarterback by a defensive end. Roc and Heat wasted no time tussling with the ballers along with Jitty and Reaper who hit them with the butt of their pistols knocking them out. They pushed them into the back seat and peeled off.

Twurk and Thang left the cookout and were now heading back home. Thang decide to call Lola to see what's up and if he should slide through. The phone rang but went to voicemail multiple times and he texted her. He has never known her to just not answer the phone or his texts unless she was sleep or something was wrong. If she was sleep she always keeps the ringer loud enough to wake her up so she could call him back. He started to get a strange feeling. "Bro, what's good? You alright?" asked Twurk seeing the worried expression on his brother's face. "Man, I don't even know! All I'm getting is the voicemail" said Thang. He took a deep breath and a hit of the loud to ease his mind. He just had this feeling that wouldn't let him be at peace.

When they got back to the house, Thang grabbed the remote to turn on the TV. He began to flip through the channels. Normally, he wouldn't be caught dead watching the news but something was telling him to not change the channel plus he recognized the area in which they were reporting. "We're reporting live, breaking news right now!" said the reporter with a somber look on his face. "There seems to have been another double homicide at the High Livings apartment complex and police suspect it may be drug related. There are two victims; both of Spanish descent. One female and one male. Both had been brutalized and fatally shot! The names of the victims are not being released yet. If anyone has any information or seen anything or anyone suspicious in the area, please call the police department with information to help bring those responsible to justice!" he ended.

Thang's mind started to run wild. "What the fuck? That can't be her!" he said to himself. He had to go see for himself.

Chapter 5

P-Murder and his crew had made it back to their spot and have forced the two ballers down into a sound proof basement. They are chained to separate steel chairs with black hoods over their heads. Their mouths were gagged and taped over with duct tape. They proceeded to work them over to get information from them. Meanwhile both their phones had been blowing up. It was Money trying to get in touch with them.

P-Murder watched the two as Roc gave them both hard body shots. "Stop! This ain't working!" said P-Murder who was standing at this point. He took a pull from the blunt as he weighed his options. "Man! Let me get at 'em! I'll make them talk with this motherfucka!" said Reaper as he cranked up the chain saw with a bugged out look on his face. "Nah! Fuck dat!" This will make them talk quick!" interrupted Jitty displaying a lit blow torch. "Y'all chill out! We gonna need them around for a few!" P-Murder told his crew in aggravation.

Thang made it to the scene and pulled into the parking area of the apartment complex. He got out and proceeded to pass by the barriers and ignored the officer's orders to stand behind the tape. He ran up to the guys carrying out a body covered in white sheets on a stretcher. When he pulled back the sheet, the face and eyes staring back at him made him almost lose his breath. He was at a loss for words.

The older male EMT that was pushing the stretcher caught wind of what Thang was experiencing and hushed the younger EMT as well as signaled the officers to stand at bay. "Sir, do you know her? Are you some kind of relative or spouse? We tried to close her eyes but they wouldn't stay close. It's as if she was waiting to see someone," he told Thang. He saw the pain in his face and immediately empathized with him. Thang was still staring down at Lola as flashbacks of all their times together came rushing back to him. "Who could have done this to Lola? And Why?" he thought to himself. "So, this is how life's hand played out for us!

Rest in Peace Babygirl!" said Thang as he fought to hold back the tears. He couldn't understand why it turned out this way. "Sir, are you related to this woman? Are you her boyfriend?" asked the EMT again.

Thang looked at the older guy then back down to Lola's eyes and eventually to the sky. "She was my first love!" he said in response. He looked at Lola one last time then ran his hands over her face leaving her eyes closed. In the background, a cop could be heard yelling, "Don't' touch the body!" but it was too late. He then went back to his truck and pulled off.

Back at home, mom and Twurk noticed that Thang was missing from the house. "Twurk, that's not like Thang to just up and leave like that! Something is wrong!" mom said. She sat down on the sofa and saw the news was on TV because Thang had left it on when he left the house. The news stations were still reporting on the murder that took place. Twurk walked over to where mom was sitting now captivated by the television. "Reporting live from High-Livings Apartment! There appears to be two victims dead at this time. Their bodies left badly beaten and mutilated. Police are saying this incident could in fact be drug-related. If anyone have any information on the killings of Lisa and Mike Vopez, please contact us at 1-800-237-9108" said the man on the TV.

Twurk walked over to where his mom was sitting captivated by the TV. He sees the footage of the apartments and the names of the dead victims go across the screen. He then became speechless as he recognized the place and the names of the victims. He also saw his brother at the scene in the background and the cameras caught every moment that Thang experienced. "What the fuck?" Twurk thought to himself as he turned to look at his mom who was now looking at him.

Thang was riding around town listening to slow songs and smoking a blunt. He was thinking about the times he and Lola shared and how he would sneak into her bedroom window with her parents asleep in the next room. He especially remembered the different positions they used to hit. He remembered mostly how she used to bite down on her pillow to keep her voice muffled when he'd hit it from the back. He'd always get a big kick out of that. He smiled to keep from crying.

In the other section of town, Money was trying to get in touch with his crew he left at the court earlier that day. He kept calling the two ballers but got no response. He wondered what could be wrong as he sniffed a line of coke. Then came a knock at the door. Money looked at Pile-Up signaling him to answer the door. Pile-Up walked to the door with his chopper in hand. Pile-Up walked back into the room where Money was with a little boy who told them a story of how he saw two of his boys getting forced into a yellow Hummer. "A yellow Hummer?" asked Money. Then he hit another line before telling Pile-Up to take care the lil boy and send him on his way. He was contemplating on what to do next as he watched the two of them leave the room.

Thang finally returned home. Twurk stopped mom from getting up when they heard the Navi pull up outside in the driveway. "Mom, stay put! I'll handle this. He turned to walk away only for mom to grab his shirt to stop him. "Baby, if anyone can get through to him, it'll have to be you," she pleaded with worried and watery eyes. Twurk understood exactly what he had to do. He nodded his head in agreement, then kissed his mom on the forehead. Before walking out the door, he turned and gave his other a smile for assurance. Thang saw Twurk as he came out of the house and stare at the windshield like he could see him through the almost presidential tinted window. "Damn! Why does this hurt so much? I guess I had more love for Lola then I knew", he thought to himself.

Thang got out of the ride, then hugged his brother who embraced him with love and concern. Mom, was staring at them from the house window. She knew exactly what Thang was feeling. She felt the same way when she lost their father. The two of them get in the Navi to ride out somewhere, they blew the horn to let mom know they were leaving. She smiled at them and waved as they drove off.

They drove around. Twurk was observing the beautiful scenery as they passed as well as the sexy women that they came upon as well. However, the image of his brother's face back at the crime scene burned in the back of his mind. He didn't say anything because he knew he had to give Thang some time to process it all. Thang lit up a blunt and leaned back into the seat as he thought about Lola and the times they shared.

Meanwhile, Pink and the crew were cruising down the highway on a mission to have some fun. "So, are we going to turn up tonight? Huh, girls? I heard the spot to do that is Club Flex! Everybody swear, it's the new hot spot!" said Pink. "Well, if it be up and popping like that, then my pussy will be up and popping in there!" said Strawberry. "Pussy poppin' on a hand stand! Ayyyeee! That's what I'm talking about!" added Choc with excitement. She was having thoughts of grinding all on Strawberry while the men and women looked at them with lust. She smiled inwardly. "Ok, I am down with Club Flex, but right now we need to get some drinks," said Peaches to her girls, shocking them since she was usually the quiet one. "What? Why y'all looking at me like I said something wrong?!" She then rolled her eyes and started back bobbing her head to the music. They stopped at the corner store. Strawberry and Choc got out to go inside. They returned minutes later with Smirnoffs for all the girls to drink. "To Club Flex!" said Choc as she raised her bottle. "To Club Flex!" they all said as they clinked their bottles together.

P-Murder and his crew were still in the basement working the two ballers. "Y'all we gonna leave these fools right here because we have other important matters to attend to," he said to his crew. "Like what? Cause I'd rather continue torturing these two!" said Heat as he pulled one of the baller's head from under the water. P-Murder took a long pull from his blunt as he stared at Heat because he knew what Heat's intentions were. "Let's not get ahead of ourselves. Trust and believe time is winding down! Believe that!" he said. They left the ballers alone and started to head upstairs. "I heard Club Flex is gonna be jumping off tonight. So, why don't we go check it out for ourselves? There's no telling who we might run into!" P-Murder told his crew as he exhaled out a cloud of smoke.

Twurk and Thang were still driving around. Thang looked up at Twurk, "Bro, we need to hit up a club tonight I have to get my mind straight," said Thang. "Shit! It's whatever, bro, but do you have a particular one in mind?" asked Twurk. Thang sat and thought for a long minute. "Yeah! This new joint called Flex!" he said as he passed the blunt to Twurk. "Dope! Let's check it out!" said Twurk. They chilled for a bit and then made their way to the club. Once there, they didn't immediately go inside because they liked to make an entrance. They just sat in the parking lot, reclined their seats and smoked a blunt while listening to music to hype themselves up for the club.

Unknowingly, Pink and her crew passed by their Navi to go inside the club. Thang recognized Strawberry out the corner of his eye just as she went inside, but he didn't tell Twurk. "You ready to go inside bro?" Twurk asked Thang. He gave a nod and the two of them finally made their way to the entrance of the club. Soon as they entered the door, they heard the Ying Yang Twin's "Wait (The Whisper Song)" blasting throughout the club.

Pink and her crew had made their way to through the club and were now settled at a table that gave them an overall view of the club. They came to have a good time, but scoping the crowds was what they usually do as they were always on the prowl.

Outside, P-Murder and his crew had just pulled up. They got out and made their way forcefully through the entrance despite resistance from one of the doorman. They each bought a bottle of Cristal and made their way through the dance floor to post up on the wall to watch the people and activity around them.

Twurk and Thang had made their way to the bar but not before checking out all the sexy ladies in attendance along the way. Before they could place their order, the bartender, Chris, and the twins, suddenly recognized each other. They all looked at each other in amazement. "Oh my God! I can't believe I'm looking at y'all two! It's been like a year and some change at least since we've seen each other back at juvie. I already know y'all want your signature drink, Red Passion. I'd still like to know how y'all came up with that one. Just in case y'all don't know, y'all are hot in these internet streets!" he said excitedly. "I went on the "Putyouon.com" website and saw that performance y'all did at Playas and Ballers. That performance was fire! Y'all have so many views and "likes", it crazy!" he added. "When y'all blow up, don't forget about lil ole me, okay? I will be y'all chauffeur, personal bartender or whatever! I just want to reap the benefits of living alongside the ones living in the spotlight and screwing famous women. I will take all the leftover women that don't make the cut! Damn! I already sound like a fucking groupie! I'll be a groupie with benefits though!" They all started laughing.

Then Chris's eyes became locked in a trance. They turned to see what he was looking at. It was Pink and her crew making their way to the bar looking like the perfect eye candy models. The Alicia Keys song, "Girl on Fire" playing in the background seemed to give them the perfect theme music. Peaches, usually being the shy & quiet type, surprisingly was the first to come directly to the bar. She couldn't believe she was this close to Twurk. The guy that had been invading her thoughts and dreams. She was now staring at him and into his sexy eyes. "Excuse me, gentlemen! I don't mean to interrupt the conversation, but if it's not too much to ask, I would to order four bottles of Moet!" said Peaches now holding eye contact with Twurk.

Twurk then remembered what his mom told him about taking the chance to converse with the girl he liked the next time he sees her. "Excuse me Miss, where I come from, men buy the first round," he said without breaking eye contact. "Is that right?" asked Peaches. "Well you must be from somewhere else, because that hardly ever happens around here!" she added. The two were definitely feeling the vibe with each other. "Maybe you've been in the wrong places!" Twurk replied.

Pink sat back observing Peaches and Twurk thinking that she is working him. Strawberry and Choc were busy vibing with one another. "That's what I'm talking about Peaches! Bring in that money!" Pink thought to herself.

P-Murder was watching what was going down between Twurk and Peaches. Thinking about he was about bring all that to an end soon. He took a drink from his bottle and he continued scoping the scene.

Back at the bar, Peaches were gathering the drinks to give to her girls. "You do know this is on the house and not just because he's playing Casanova, but I owe him a favor for saving my life once. You are looking at a legend and soon to be music mogul right here!" said Chris. Peaches then looked from Chris and back to Twurk. "Thanks for the information!" she said trying to sound unimpressed. She grabbed the ice bucket and the four bottles of Moet and turned to leave. She stopped suddenly to say, "Oh Yeah! Maybe I wasn't looking at all Romeo! Thanks for the drinks!" she said with a smile. Peaches and her girls headed back to their table. She placed the bucket on the table and took her seat. She noticed that all the girls were now looking at her curiously. "What? Y'all thought I lost my groove or something? Never that!" she said as she then grabbed a bottle. That was when she noticed the four champagne glasses inside the bucket. She smiled inside at Twurk's charming craftiness. She then poured herself a drink.

Back at the wall, Reaper spotted the girls then tapped Heat on the shoulder and pointed to Pink. "Ain't that her?" he asked. Heat stopped drinking to look in the direction Reaper was pointing. "Yeah! "That's her!"

Pink was now feeling the effects from the Moet along with her girls as they were all drinking, singing, dancing and having a good time. "I don't know about y'all, but I'm going to get my groove on! Y'all gonna just sit there and look pretty, or are y'all gonna get loose on the dance floor?" she asked as she danced to the music. "We with you, girl!" said Choc and Strawberry as they headed to the floor. Pink then glanced back at Peaches and noticed her quietness. "Girl, you alright? Don't tell me that bottle got the best of you already!" she said playing along like her girl isn't really falling for Mr. Green eyes at the bar. "Yeah! I'm straight, girl! Y'all go and have fun! Seriously, I'm ok!" Peaches assured Pink but knowing full well she wasn't. She watched as they made their way to the dance floor.

Roc saw Pink on the dance floor and headed her way. He walked up on Pink from behind. "Excuse me, ma! Can I have this dance?" he asked while licking his lips.

Chapter 6

"Who the fuck?" Oh! Shit! You better start being more careful! Walking all up on me like that! I done seen plenty of people get shot doing the shit you just did!" said Pink to Roc. "My bad!" said Roc as he examined her body language. He saw this was the perfect time and opportunity to get close to her again. "Damn! I see this is the only way that I can get up with you!" he said as he licked his lips and gave a smile. Pink, then cocked her head to the side with a hand on her hip and the other hand inches away from Roc's face. This signals him to stop in his tracks. "First & foremost, I done my part by giving you my number! You should have used it! You must have been too busy entertaining some of your little hoochies or something!" said Pink to Roc with a fake angry, and seductive look on her face.

Roc, being the type that feeds off of this type of feedback, stepped toward Pink and placed his hands on her slim waist as he slowly pulled her close to him. "You know how it is, when you're in them streets," he said charmingly. "But I do assure you that I meant no harm and I do apologize," he said as he smiled making sure to lay his game on thick.

Since game recognize game, Pink peeped what was going on, but it still was a turn on. "Tonight, is a good night!" she said to Roc. "Why don't we just enjoy ourselves?" she added as she rested the side of her face on his Versace shirt. She ran her hands up and down his back all the while wondering to herself just how much he was worth. Roc decided to see if her ass was as soft as it looked. He glided both his hands along its roundness and then palmed her cheeks. This sent a rush of sensation to his hardening penis. "Too bad my homie wants her dead! Damn! I've got to hit this before he makes the final hit!" he thought to himself as they slow danced to the music.

Strawberry and Choc were dancing together all seductively in such a manner that one would expect the removal of clothes to follow. P-Murder and his crew were peeping the action. "Man, those two chicks must be a couple or something? I gots to find out for myself! I'll be right back. Y'all fellas watch a playa work!" said Jitty as he winked at Reaper to signal the competition has begun. "You ain't saying nothing! I bet you a hundred dollars, I'll get the panties before you do!" said Reaper accepting the challenge. "P, big bruh, you're the witness to what's about to go down!" Reaper told P-Murder. They both headed towards Strawberry and Choc.

Heat somehow found his way to the table where Peaches was sitting. He slid into the seat, which took her by surprise. He took a sip from his bottle of Cristal all while continuously watching her. The look on his face was menacing. Peaches, now feeling the heat fueled by anger coming from his direction and she knew exactly why, finally says, "Excuse me, but do I owe you anything?" trying to play him to the left.

Heat then slammed the bottle down hard on the table, which made Peaches jump at the sound of it. "Bitch! Do you fucking see stupid written on my forehead or something? This is what the fuck I am talking about!" he added as he slammed the fake number down on the table. Peaches still pretended not to know what was his issue and everything was fine. Heat feeling even more frustrated decide to pull out his nine and put it on the table. This intensified the moment instantly. Peaches knew that if she says the wrong thing, it might be at risk of her getting killed. In her mind, he had now escalated from a "lame" to a maniac. This was the time if ever for her to think quick. She kept telling herself to stay calm wait to make her move as she stared at Heat with his hand on the trigger and the barrel of the gun pointed at her.

From the bar, Twurk observed to be a tense moment between Heat and Peaches. He recognized him as being the guy she was dancing with the other night and it made him a little salty. He still felt something wasn't right with their interaction, but his now bitter feelings kept him from exploring further. Thang also noticed the interaction between the two of them and was ready to do whatever his brother wanted at any given moment. "Bro, ain't that the same chick you just bought them bottles of Moet for earlier?" asked Thang. Twurk took a drink. "Yeah, that is her with that guy from the other night," he said disappointedly. "If that is who she is fucking with, I feel sorry for her," he added. "That guy looks like he is a women beater or some kind of deranged lunatic," said Thang.

"Well if that's the type of men she be attracting, then that's on her!" We are here to celebrate tonight. So, to us!" he said as he proclaimed a toast. Twurk tried to play it off as if he wasn't feeling Peaches anymore but Thang knew the truth.

Jitty and Reaper have caught up with Strawberry and Choc on the dance floor. "What's up, shawty? Y'all two are looking so damn good together. Me and man here are trying to get with the two of you tonight. I'm really really trying to get with you!" Jitty said as he stepped closer to Strawberry. He was confident in the game he was spittin' especially with the help from Cristal and the dro' he was smoking on. Strawberry, a bit intrigued by his courage and humorous way of approach, just looked him up and down as to size him up and find out what he's working with. She paused for a second and then looked him in the eyes. "I feel where you're coming from, but if my girl ain't feeling ya man over there, then I ain't feeling you!" she said with a smirk on her face.

Reaper, now feeling the pressure, decided it was now or never. He stepped up to Choc in a forceful yet seducing manner. "What's up ma? Can Mr. Reaper have this dance to this lovely song? Cause I do believe this song was meant for you and I in this moment," he said. Choc seemed a bit hesitant. "Please, don't make me go grab the microphone and beg you over the speakers because I will do it! I'll go right now if you don't believe me. Just watch me!" he insisted as he began to walk off towards the mic. Before he could take a second step, he felt a tug pulling him back. "Bingo!" he thought to himself knowing that he now had her on his hook.

Choc gave Strawberry a wink as she laughed at Reaper who thinks he has her in the palm of his hands. "You are so damn funny! Come on! I can't turn you down, even if I wanted too," she told Reaper. "So, I guess tonight is my lucky night!" said Jitty to Strawberry reminding her of the conditions. "I can also do the robot, the waltz, the boxtrot and the salsa!" he added and they both started laughing as he does his best impression of the robot. "Boy! You are a plum fool! Stop, you got everyone looking at us!" Jitty started doing the salsa and she laughs again but this time she also put her hands around his neck and joined him.

At the bar, Thang was still eyeing the situation at the table with Peaches and Heat. "Aye bro, I ain't the smartest person in the world but I think your girl over there may be in some trouble," he told his brother as he took a hit off a blunt. "Like I said before, if that's who she chooses to deal with, that is her problem. Plus, she's not my girl!" replied Twurk still trying to deny his feelings. Peaches could be seen staring at Heat with her eyes like flames of fire. She wanted to turn the tables on him so bad. She knew there was always bad karma out there waiting for her and she'd have to pay but she didn't think it would be over some damn number.

"Yo! Check this out!" Heat insisted as he leaned closer. "This is how we're gonna do this. You and I are gonna get up and walk out of here. If you make any false moves, I'm gonna blow you're fucking head off! Don't even think about playing with me! Comprende?" he said forcefully through clenched teeth. He stopped to take a drink of Cristal. Peaches watched Heat turn up the bottle and then seized her opportunity. She then, turned the table over towards Heat, which caught him off guard, as she crouched low and took off running through the crowded dance floor.

. "Fucking bitch! I'll kill you!" he shouted. After gaining his composure, Heat did a quick spin and fired off two shots at Peaches as she fled. He missed but now has the attention of the whole club and has lost sight of Peaches. At this point he didn't care about that or if he hit someone mistakenly trying to fire at Peaches. All he saw was red. The crowd around was fleeing and ducking, while some people were getting trampled over trying to find the nearest exit or hiding spot from the bullets.

Twurk who heard the shots and recognized the source from which they came. He realized that Peaches must be in danger. The mixture of the alcohol, blunts and emotions caused him to move without really thinking or scoping out the place. He pulled out his .45 and started to head towards Heat.

P-Murder, peeping the move that Twurk is about to make, smiled with pleasure as the perfect opportunity for payback has presented itself. "Rest in peace green eyes!" said P-Murder to himself as he sent five shots in Twurk's direction. They hit like a ton of bricks one by one in the stomach area of Twurk's body. Thang watched in disbelief as he saw his brother shot. He thought that maybe the alcohol and the blunts were making him see things, but quickly snapped back into the reality that this really happened. He pulled his .45 and started scoping through the crowd. He thought he saw who pulled the trigger so he began shooting. His vision was blurry from the blunt and alcohol so he missed. Fortunately, he missed the innocent bystanders too. He looked back to see his brother lying in a puddle of blood and appears to be out cold.

P-Murder and his crew immediately dipped out of the club without hesitation. It seemed like protocol for them, because bullets popping off in the club was highly likely to be coming from one or more members of their crew. Soon as the first shot was let off, they were on the move. After P-Murder shot Twurk they all exited the club and were back into their ride and on the road in no time. "Heat! What the fuck was you thinking about man? I know you didn't let that bitch get to you like that!" said P-Murder glaring over at Heat. "Man, fuck that bitch! She should have never played me like that. I ain't gon' stop until I kill that bitch!" Heat replied as he locked eyes with P-Murder.

Pink, being as acclimated to the streets as she is, made sure to remain low and scanned the club for her girls. She spotted Strawberry and Choc and then made her way over to them. "Yo! Where's Peaches?" she asked them. "We can't leave without her! We came together, we leave together!" she added. "I saw a glimpse of her earlier as she went running outside. I think that guy was shooting at her. I hope she alright!' said Strawberry. They made their way out of the club being cautious along the way.

Thang and Chris carried Twurk out of the club and put him in the backseat of the Navi. Chris rode in back with Twurk who was bleeding badly at this point as Thang sped off to the hospital. "Hold on bruh! You gonna make it! Just hold on!" Thang said to Twurk. "God, please don't let my bro die?" he thought to himself.

Peaches was outside the club hiding between cars and waiting to spot her girls leave. She saw as Thang and Chris put Twurk's bloody body in the backseat and pulled off, which frightened her a bit more. She finally spotted them as they were looking wildly about to locate her. She wanted to call out to them but given what just happened and she doesn't know the whereabouts of Heat she remained quiet. Strawberry suddenly spotted her, "Oh my God! There goes Peaches over there!" she said to the other girls. Pink came up to Peaches and looked her girl over. She realized that she was okay, but still a little shaken up about things. She glanced around at everyone else still running to their vehicles and peeling off and decided they should do the same.

Peaches now in the backseat is hearing sirens getting closer so could Pink. So, they took the back way to avoid traffic and cops. Peaches' mind keeps playing back to the image of Twurk being hauled away and the things she wishes she did but didn't say. She is left with the possible feeling that he might pass away. She hoped that what happened to him had nothing to do with her. She closed her eyes and said a prayer for him and opened them only to see Pink's eyes staring back at her in the rearview mirror.

En route to the hospital Thang is running red lights and pushing the Navi as fast as it can go. He even had to weave through traffic on the interstate praying they don't get into an accident along the way. The incident plays back over in his mind. He knew something was not right with the chick and the dude at the table he just couldn't figure it out. All hell just broke loose but what messed him up the most was he couldn't figure out who or where the shots came from. He made a vow that when he did find out, he would kill them. He pulled into the hospital's parking lot are not far from the front of the emergency room. He and Chris took Twurk out the back seat and headed towards the entrance. They were met by nurses who got Twurk safely on to the stretcher then hurriedly took him down the hall and disappeared through the double doors.

"Sir! Are you alright? I take it that is your brother?" said one of the nurses to Thang trying to keep him from following the stretcher. "You and your friend will have to wait out here in the waiting room and let us do our jobs to help your brother. Just be patient and continue praying for him to pull through? Soon as I know what's going on I will inform you," said the nurse as they headed through the double doors. Chris was hoping he would have helped saved Twurk's life by helping him get to the hospital since Twurk saved his life long ago when he defaulted on a gambling debt. He prayed that Twurk would pull through.

Pink and the crew made it home and Peaches was thoroughly exhausted and she couldn't do much but just go to bed. As the water from the shower head massaged her body, all she could think of was Twurk. She prayed silently for God to be with him.

Back at the hospital, Thang was pacing back and forth while Chris sat in the waiting room chair dozing off periodically. Thang started to get heated all over again. "Man, I don't give a fuck! Whoever did this to my brother is gonna pay!" he yelled as he punched the wall. Then he went back to pacing while punching the inside of his palm. In the back, the doctors were working hard to save Twurk. He had flatlined a couple of times but they managed to bring him back. Relieved they were able to resuscitate him they were getting him prepped for surgery.

The doctor came out to talk to Thang. Thang walked over to the doctor and immediately asked him about the condition of his brother, which woke up Chris who immediately joined Thang to find out Twurk's condition. "Tell me Doc! Is my bro alright? Where is he? Can I see 'em?" Thang asked the doctor.

"Son, please calm down! I know how you feel, trust me. The only thing we can do is pray and wait. Your brother is in good hands. We thought we were going to lose him, but he pulled through. Right now, he is about to undergo surgery in a few. Your brother is definitely a fighter! Have a little faith. That's all you can do now. It is best to just go home and get a good rest. If anything changes we will give you a call. You have my word! Thang was hesitant but eventually gave in to the doctor's suggestion. He and Chris walked off.

Twurk, now unconscious, slips into the dream world where he saw his father. "Yo dad! Is that really you?" he asked. "Man, it's so good to see you, playa! Why are you dressed up like an angel?" His father then touched him on the shoulder and stared him in the face realizing how much he had grown since he last saw him. "Son, do you know where you are? You are one step closer to the afterlife!" he told Twurk which immediately sent a look of shock over his face. Then it all started to make sense of how everything looked and his father having angel wings. "The afterlife? Does that mean I'm dead?" "Not quite yet! It's not your time!" his dad replied. Twurk was somewhat relieved because he was not quite ready to go. "Just kick it for a little while with your old pops!"

Thang dropped Chris off and was on the way home. He was wondering how he was supposed to begin to tell his mom about what happened to Twurk. He just couldn't. So, he didn't go home. He went to Pop's Car Wash to clean all the blood out of the Navi. After he was done cleaning, he got a call from a number he didn't recognize. "Hello, this Thang! Who the fuck is this?" then he heard the hospital intercom go off in the background and realized that it was the doctor. "Tell me something good, doc? How is my brother doing?" asked Thang. The doctor hearing the urgency in his voice told him "Your brother's condition looks to be improving. The surgery went fine. He will need lots of rest though. I advise you to get some rest as well. He should be able to have visitors tomorrow. You and your family should be able to see him. In the meantime, go comfort them," he insisted. "Ok Doc! I'm trusting you to make sure my bro good, ok?" said Thang. "Tell my brother I'm coming to visit him soon!" he added. "I will do just that! You get some rest!" said the doctor and with that he ended the conversation.

"Damn! I gots to go home and break the news to mom! I know she is going to flip out!" he thought to himself. Suddenly the phone rang. It's mom. "Hello!" he answered with hesitation. Mom had saw the news on TV called Thang. "Baby! Did you see the news?" she asked as she begin to cry. "Tell me! Tell me my Twurk ain't dead? Why didn't you call me? Where are you? Come home now! I need you here! Please, baby! Just come home!" said mom to Thang who couldn't get a word in edge wise. "Mom, don't worry! I'm coming home. Please stop crying! I am on my way home now. I love you mom!" said Thang as he hung up the phone.

Chapter 7

P-Murder at the crib sitting in his usual spot in a chair by the window contemplating the next moves. He realized Heat was becoming too reckless with his vendetta against Peaches. Although it did set up the perfect opportunity, it was not something that went according to plan. Just then, a news report came on the television that caught his attention. The reporter stated that an anonymous tip had come in involving the abduction of two men from the basketball courts. The tipster reported that two young men by the name of Terrance "Juice" Metz and Chris "Grillz" Myin were chased, beaten, and kidnapped by some black males in a yellow Hummer. No names had been given of the suspects and so far, the authorities didn't have any leads. The reporter urged if anyone had any information to call 1-800 –55-CRIME.

P-Murder relieved that there was no solid information tying them to the crime also realized that this was just more heat they didn't need and they need to be more careful. He decided it was high time to go check on his two guests.

Thang and mom were moving swiftly in the morning with the anticipation of seeing Twurk. The doctor had called earlier to report that Twurk was stable and strong so their visit this morning should be exactly what he needs to push him to a speedy recovery. "Mom! We need to hurry up and get ready so we can see Twurk!" said Thang to mom as he was rushing to the shower. "No, you need to hurry!" said mom. "I'm already two steps ahead of you!" she added while looking at her outfit in the mirror. Once they were both dressed they made their way to the hospital.

They reached the entrance with anticipation and made their way to the lobby elevator where two women got off once the elevator doors opened. One was a pretty caramel complexioned honey who locked eyes with Thang and made sure to put a jiggle in her step as she walked by. Thang almost walked to follow her out like he was under the spell of the pied piper until mom snatched him back to reality and the current reason for visiting the hospital. Mom looked at him with disappointment to which he apologized. They got on the elevator and Thang pressed the button to the fifth floor.

Mom, not knowing what to expect when she sees Twurk, continued the elevator ride in silence and mental anguish. "God, please give me strength! Please bring my Twurk back home with me! Let this also be an eye-opener for them," she thought to herself. She then glanced over at Thang who seemed to be in deep thought himself. For Thang, memories from the club that night plus the way he lost Lola kept playing over and over in his mind. He began to think that it couldn't just be coincidence and that someone must have it out for him and his brother, but he couldn't think of who it could be.

The ding from the elevator seemed to pull him out of his trance. The doors opened and as they got off the elevator, the doctor was there to greet them. "Good morning! This must be your sister!" he says trying to charm mom and lighten the mood for her given the circumstances. She smiles and laughs softly. She took a deep breath and exhaled to prepare to see her son. She introduced herself to the doctor and told him that although she was flattered, she was most definitely their mother. Thang, now anxious, asked if they could go see Twurk now. The doctor, seeing the anticipation and impatience on his face, obliged. "Right this way!" he said as they begin to make their way to Twurk's room.

Pink and her crew were still worn out from the previous night's events. Pink, who was the only one awake, had just got up to take a shower. Passing by Strawberry and Choc's room, she saw them all cuddled up in bed together. She then closed the door shut and continued down the hall after shaking her head at them. "Those two are off the chain, but they're my girls and I love them!" she thought to herself as she entered her room. The closing of the door had awakened Choc a little. She felt

Strawberry's warm presence and slight movements. She ran her hand gently up and down Strawberry's smooth, bare back.

Strawberry eyes opened to look at Choc removing a strand of her black hair from her face. "Good morning! You look so beautiful and desirable in the morning, boo!" Strawberry told Choc. She caressed Choc's face then moved down to her nipples now hard from the stimulation. She took one into her mouth while caressing the other one with aggressive pleasure. Hearing sexy moans escape Choc's lips turned her on. She planted kisses and licked her way down stopping short of Choc's now wet cookie and placed her fingers inside of her. "Mmm! My baby stay wet. Let mama taste you, baby!" she said just before spreading Choc's legs far apart then sliding her tongue over her pierced clit and into where her fingers once were. Choc loves the tongue action Strawberry is giving her so she grabs the back of her head to ensure she hits all the right spots. Getting more turned on by the moans from Choc, Strawberry starts pleasuring herself with the same rhythm she is giving Choc. They both begin to moan with pleasure until they climaxed.

Peaches sitting in front of her mirror in the next room heard the screams of ecstasy. She stopped brushing her hair to make sure what she was hearing. She only smiled and giggled softly then went right back to brushing her hair. She was thinking about Twurk and the events at the club. She could see him standing behind her as her thoughts were that strong. Her breathing got heavier as he got closer. Her breast swelled and nipples hardened as he caressed her face. She moaned at the intensity of the pulsing and wetness that came as he kissed her neck. She anticipated what was to come, when a loud knock at her door snapped her back into reality. It was Pink. Apparently, she had been knocking while Peaches was deep in her trance. "It's open!" said Peaches. "Peaches! Girl are you alright? Didn't you hear me knocking? What's really going with you? Ever since that night you've been distant!" said Pink being like the big sister she usually is. However, Peaches did not want them to worry or think she was going crazy, so she gave her a big smile and assured her that she was ok. She said she just needed time alone to process it all but appreciate the love and concern. "I'm okay for real. I know you heard those two getting' freaky just a while ago!" she said as she laughed trying to change the subject and show that she was okay even if she wasn't. "Just give me a few minutes, then I will be out," she added trying to get rid of Pink to get back to finish the scene playing out in her mind before Pink knocked on the door. "Okay, girl!" said Pink. "This morning was nothing; you should have heard them last night!" she added. They both laughed as Pink left the room.

Considering the events over the past few days, P-Murder called a round table meeting to get all the crew together. They all were sitting around smoking and drinking while waiting on P-Murder to break the uncomfortable silence. P-Murder took a sip and placed his drink down on the table. "Alright! We know the two fools in the basement are connected to the Haitian. Something in my gut tells me one of those lil' punks will eventually talk if we applied the right amount of pressure," he said. "So, what you're saying is that you want us to turn it up a notch?" asked Heat. "You know all I need is a blow torch and ten minutes with them punks. They will be more than ready to cooperate then," he added meaning every word. P-Murder watched Heat as he talked. Although, he wanted to silence him from the reckless stunt he pulled prior, he didn't because he believed Heat may be on to something. "If you're right about this Heat, you might just get a promotion!" said P-Murder raising his drink to toast but he didn't mean a word he just said at all since Heat has been a liability lately. "Let's get to work!" said P-Murder to his boys.

They made their way to the basement and figured they should start with the shorter one first. They started yelling at them telling them they better start talking about the Haitians, their connections, or where's the money. P-Murder slapped them both. Heat readies his blow torch and P-Murder notices the taller one's legs start to quiver and immediately he knew he would be the one to break first. All of a sudden, his phone starts to ring. He took the call and raises a single hand to his crew to halt their mission. "Yo! Something just came up. We will take care of these two when we get back! Let's take a ride!" said P-

Murder. They all depart the basement leaving the two ballers in the darkness.

With Twurk in the hospital, Red and Five had been trying to get in touch with Thang to find out his condition. They only got the voicemail time and time again. Five was really affected by what happened to Twurk. He stared out of the window at the ocean in his beachfront house. He was watching the people on the beach but interrupted by hands placed lightly on his abs that glided down to his manhood. It was his girl, Faith, who was bringing him a fresh squeezed glass of orange juice. "Thanks!" he said as he planted a kiss on her soft, glossy lips. He turned to look out at the water again.

Faith massaged the muscles in his neck and then started to kiss it softly as to comfort him. "So, what is on your mind so heavily? Have you heard anything more on Twurk's condition? I know it has to be talking a toll on their mom and his brother," said Faith sounding concerned. She took a look at the people having fun on the beach and looked at him. "Baby, don't worry yourself too hard! Cause momma needs some of your time!" she said staring at him. "Like now!" she whispered in his ear while her hands cradled his rock-hard manhood as she maneuvered him over to the bed and pushed him down with a smile.

At the hospital, Thang and his mom were visiting with Twurk in his room. Mom placed her hands onto Twurk's hands and stood looking down at him trying not to cry. She knew Twurk was not perfect but sleeping like he was he looked just like an angel to her. The moment triggered flashbacks of when she last saw Twurk at the house and the last time she saw their father. She was hoping that her son did not meet the same fate and that he would soon come home to her. She turned to Thang and told him to come closer so they could say a prayer together. "Oh, heavenly Father!" she started. "Let not my words of prayer and petition be in vain and my heart be uncleansed. I know my son hasn't been a saint, but I know you are full of mercy and grace. Please bring my son back to me. I've already lost their father and can't bare another loss this close. Please Father, don't take my Twurk! It is in your name we ask and pray! Amen!" she ended as she opened her eyes and glanced towards the heavens. She then looks Thang in the eyes and tells him, "Son! I love you both, but whatever you two are doing out there in them streets, please stop. I can't bear the thought of losing y'all. I put the two of you in the Father's hands because I'm not there with you everywhere you go but He can be!" she said wiping her eyes with a handkerchief.

Twurk, although unconscious can hear the words of his mother to him and Thang. Twurk smiles as the words of his mother comfort him. His father also hearing the words told Twurk that he misses their mother and have missed a lot that he should have been there. He tells Twurk that he has to realize what he has in his mom and his brother and that he has to go and be there for them since he can't. He tells Twurk to always remember him and that he loved them all. He hugged Twurk and began to fade away.

Mom, now sitting with her eyes closed, seemed to be deep in meditation and prayer. Suddenly, she felt her and being squeezed. "Twurk! Did you just squeeze my hand? Oh my God! Thang! Thang, I think Twurk just squeezed my hand!" she shouted. "Look! He's waking up!" She began to weep with joy. Thang tried to keep his composure as they learned from their father to keep their displays of emotions to a minimum. "Never show weakness and never let anyone see you cry! Never!" he told them. When he saw that his brother had fully regained consciousness, he only gave him a head nod to relay all the things he couldn't show emotionally.

Twurk looked at the both of them standing there at his bedside. "Mom! How are you? Glad to see you too bro!" he said in a low voice. Twurk then starts coughing and grunts as he tried to sit up. He didn't make it all the up so he fell back onto the bed. He was still kind of drowsy and weak from the sedatives. He took a deep breath and exhaled as he rested. Thang trying to show him some tough love told him, "So you mean to tell me, you're going to let some bullets and medicine hold you down? Man, you better get your ass up out of that bed. I got these bad ass shawties waiting on us!" he said thinking that would motivate Twurk. "Plus, I heard the club is jumping tonight!" he added. "Ouch! What was that for?" he said as mom pinched him hard on the arm. "Your brother hasn't been awake five whole minutes from being shot and fighting for his life! And here you are trying to take him back to the same place that got him here! I don't think so!" she told Thang. "Twurk, I am putting you on house restriction! That goes for you too young man!" she said smiling and pointing at Thang. She begun to get a glimpse of that old family feeling they used to have and it comforted her. Twurk just smiled at the two of them as he also remembered the brief moment he spent with his father. Coincidentally, mom was also thinking of T-Red in this moment. She just happened to glance over at the door to see the doctor peeping through the door window so she waved at him to come inside. He walked in and felt the spirits were high in the room and he gave a smile. "I see the warrior has finally awakened!" he said as he took a sip of his coffee and look at his chart. He gave Twurk a wink and flashed a smile. Mom walked towards him. "Doctor!" she said with a smile on her face and in her eyes. "Call me Charlie!" he insisted. "Charlie! Thank you so much for saving my boy!" she said staring into his eyes. Thang peeped the smile on his mom's face and the energy they were giving off. He was having none of it. The doctor, now feeling Thang's eyes peering at him, shifted the mood of the moment by focusing on Twurk. "Well, he is in stable condition, but recovering and needs his rest. So, I'm going to have to ask you two to wrap it up soon so my patient can get his rest and fully recover," he said as he pat Twurk on the leg. "You definitely are more the welcome to come back tomorrow!" he said looking directly at mom. He turned to walk toward the door when Thang approached him as if he was going to mention the interaction between him and his mom, but instead he thanked him for saving his brother as he attempted to dap him up. Thang laughed because it took him a minute to catch the rhythm.

Chapter 8

Money, along with two of his most trusted comrades, Killa and Murda, went strolling around the park early in the morning where they typically do a lot of their plotting. He sensed a strange feeling in the air and thought the birds felt the same because they seem to behave different. He took a seat on the bench with Killa and Murda sitting on opposite sides of him. He decided to try Juice's cell one more time but still couldn't get an answer. He came to the conclusion that Juice and Grillz were still being held hostage or dead. Juice was one of the key players in his organization that he fully trusted and he looked after him like a son. Money especially didn't want to waste any time to get to the bottom of what happened. He called Pile-Up to get the first move going to handle the situation. "Pile-Up! Put the word out for da 411 on that yellow humma! I still haven't been able to reach them. This has to be handled immediately!" and with that he hung up the phone. He got up from the bench and stretched his hands to the sky, which was his way of flexing like a king. The sun shone brightly on his dark tinted lenses and out of nowhere four black crows landed in his path. Money, just smiled devilishly and walked off but not before throwing some plastic object on the ground. "Something for the crows!" he said as he laughed and walked away.

Pile-Up made calls to all the usual suspects that were considered the eyes and ears on the streets. He heard the door open and in walked Money with Killa and Murder. He greeted Money then bent down to give Killa and Murda a good scratching on the tops of their heads and sent them on to another part of the house. He began to tell Money any information he happened to find out. Money is convinced that there is no more to be said only bodies to count when they catch up with whomever is responsible.

Feeling like he had made some progress, he went to go shower. As steam filled up the room, Money stood at the sink looking at the mirror. On the sink, he had his gold plate with a small pile of coke which he separated into four lines. He cleared two lines before rising to stare back at his reflection in the mirror. He saw a younger version of his father, known as the king of Haiti's streets. "Damn Pa! Me looks just like ya! Ya all me have left in this life, goin to have to visit ya soon! Me gon' coke and kill till me die just like ya! Fuck this land! Haiti pride forever!" He cleared the last two lines of coke and got in the shower.

Pile-Up was lounging in the living room when he got a call on his phone. He answered. "Who dis?" he asked not recognizing the number. "Me got some good news!" said the voice on the other end. "Dem guys, Dey are known as P-Murder's crew! P-Murder and his crew drive that yellow humma ya lookin' for! Me don't know the whereabouts yet, but P-Murder definitely be the one ya lookin' for! Me let you know if something else turn up! Haiti Pride!" he yelled. "Good lookin' out!" said Pile-Up before ending the call. He walked down the hall passing by Killa and Murda who always stood guard, to give Money the good news.

Thang grew restless around the house. He was trying to not constantly think about what happened to Twurk but trying to figure out who would be responsible for the five shots and coming up empty frustrated him even more. He took a slow pull of the blunt and decided to call Five to see what he was up to. "Helloo! Who may this be?" said Faith in a sexy voice pretending not to see the Caller ID. He immediately knew who it was and immediately got hard. Faith was a pure sex nympho that always craved him and he couldn't resist her. The first time they hooked up, Five had just ran off to go handle business at the club but left Thang at his place to mix some music. Faith, sensing that Five had left, entered the living room where Thang was wrapped in just a towel pretending as if she was headed to take a shower. He couldn't help but notice how thick and curvaceous she was but tried to ignore the temptation because Five was his homie after all. Faith knew he was tempted to touch so walked over to him and pretended to try to clear the glasses that they had been using so she squeezed between him and the bar. When she was directly in front of Thang she leaned back into him grinding slowly. He seemed to be hypnotized by the site of her round, plump booty. She then leaned on the bar and pushed back harder onto Thang's midsection. He didn't know what to do, but couldn't move because the feeling was too good. She started moaning and then looked back at Thang. Her eyes inviting him in as she bit her bottom lip. "Time is ticking, big daddy! Give momma what she's been missing!" she said seductively as she blew him a kiss. His mind was telling him no because of his loyalty to Five and the trust he had in him, but his body was saying just the opposite. In the end, this was the first of their secret trysts together. Thang remembered how Faith moaned his name and every position they were in. It had him deep in thought. "Don't tell me some kid is playing on my fucking phone!" screamed Faith bringing Thang back to the present. "Thang is that you!" she yelled. "Yeah! Who the fuck you talking to like that?" he asked trying to play it off like he wasn't just off in La La Land. "You better tone down your voice when you talking to me, ma! My brother in the hospital, fools trying to kill me and...Just save the attitude, okay!

Faith giggled to herself as she took a sip of Red Passion. "Yeah! Yeah! Yeah! I done heard a lot of big talk and no action. You gone have to come better than that! You sound scared or something!" she said testing his manhood.

"Scared? Bitch please! I run the streets! My brother is recovering in the hospital cause some pussy boy tried to take his life! I got too much on my plate right now!" said Thang as he tried to calm his nerves by taking another hit of the blunt. "I got your bitch! So, you mean to tell me that the Almighty Thang is worrying about someone else for a change? I thought you would've been getting busy with your best friend's wifey! Damn! Don't tell me you're going all soft! You know momma likes it real hard," she said as she laughed. "Seriously, I don't want to hear no excuses about your brother being in the hospital, or somebody trying to kill you! Come kill this pussy! That's what you need to do!" she said insistently. "Are you coming over or not?" she asked as she took another sip from her glass and bit her lower lip. She also hung up the phone and smiled to herself seeing how easy it was to get Thang all riled up and lure him over to her almost every time. She knew he would come.

Thang pulled up to Five's spot with the music low as he would usually do when he's in creep mode. He downed one mini bottle of Red Passion before making his way to the entrance.

Before he could knock on the door, it opened. There stood Faith in the doorway wearing a burgundy silk robe while carrying a party-sized bottle of Red Passion and two glasses. She smiled seductively as she said, "Come get it, tiger!" Thang took one look at her and licked his lips in amazement. The blunts and the liquor mixed together in his system has him relaxed but extra excited at the same time. It was something about Faith. She was the one piece of pussy he couldn't seem to get enough of, even at the expense of his best friend finding out. Thang crossed the threshold of the doorway and with one swift tug he undid the bathrobe to reveal Faith's naked body. Her skin was soft as butter and the tone, a smooth caramel complexion that glistened in the light. This made Thang even more ready to give her what she's been waiting for. He planted his mouth on one of her breasts as he cuffed her ass aggressively, just how she liked it. He ended up lifting her off the ground so she wrapped her arms around his neck and her legs around his waist. He closed the door behind them with a swift back kick as they made their way upstairs to Faith's playroom. They were kissing each other so hard they damn near pulled out each other's tongues as they got more and more excited with each step they climbed.

Meanwhile Five was on his way to get a special something for his lady, Faith. He pulled up to the Forever Jewels store in his custom fire red jag with burgundy wood grain interior. As he makes his way to the store entrance he saw an old neighborhood friend who was down on his luck and handed him a few crispy hundred dollar bills. "God bless you!" said the man.   Five entered the store. He is met with the smell of fresh roses and other fragrant scents with some soft music playing in the background. As all heads turn in his direction he makes sure to keep his business face on when deep down he wanted to ask them "what the fuck are you looking at?" He almost let it slip but kept his composure. The store manager, who bared a striking resemblance to Ricky Martin, approached him to assist him.

"Hello! My name is Weasly! What can I do for you today?" he asked Five. "Hello, I am here today looking for a special ring for my special lady!" Five replied. "Right this way!" he said as he motioned for Five to follow him to the display of rings. Five settled on a halo diamond engagement ring because he was sure that Faith was his angel. It was 18k white gold-metal with round cut diamonds around the band and in a circle around a center diamond piece. "I'll take this one!" said Five. He paid cash for it and left the store.

Thang and Faith had just finished their third round of their sex session. They were lying on top of the sheets panting, trying to catch their breaths. Thang was contemplating on the idea of Five and Faith tying the knot and how twisted it was since Faith is nothing but a deceptive nympho that's probably only in it for the money. Faith rolled onto her side, making sure to have skin to skin contact with Thang. She started rubbing on his abs to bring him back to reality as she saw he was in a daze. "Thang! Snap out of it! I need you here, not in outer space somewhere! I want for us to finally--!" she stopped as Thang put his finger over her lips to silence her.

He looked into her eyes and could see that whatever she was about to say, she was also serious about. Since he was not trying to be serious with her at all, he just played it off. "I know you do! We gotta have a little more patience! Trust me; when the time is right, we'll both be happy in the end," he told her with a smile on his face. He started kissing her passionately but aggressively while caressing her breasts. She then put her hands onto his chest and pushed him on his back as she straddled him. She started massaging his chest, abs and worked her way down to his manhood. "You like this baby?" she asked as she made him as stiff as a board. He didn't answer but she saw it in his eyes. So she takes her lips and kisses tip before taking it further into her mouth as she glides up and down slurping and sucking with each upward movement. She massages his testicles with one of her hands. Thang groaned with pleasure.

Meanwhile, outside, Red had just pulled up to the house. He

realized that Five's jag was gone but Twurk and Thang's Navi was there. So, he thought they were inside. He thought that maybe Faith had taken the jag to go shopping, leaving the guys at the house to their usual antics. He walked up to the door and rung the bell, which caused Faith to almost choke. "Oh shit! Who the fuck is that?" she said with her heart beating fast. She leaped over Thang to go over to the window and peek through the curtains. All Thang saw was titties and ass jiggling which made him chuckle a bit in the middle of being nervous about getting caught up. "It's Red's fucking ass! I will handle him so don't you go anywhere! I am definitely not done with you yet!" said Faith as she blew him a kiss and headed towards the door. Just before she made it out, Thang jumped out of the bed and grabbed her from behind. He started kissing her on the neck and squeezing her breasts. "You better hurry back!" he whispered in her ear before smacking her on the ass. She grabbed her robe from off the floor and hurried out of the room. He went over to the window to peek out. He saw Red at the door. "Red and that stupid ass hair do!" he said as he laid back in the bed.

Red was starting to get impatient, because it shouldn't take them this long to answer the door. He tried to look through the peep hole to see any commotion. He was about to turn and leave when Faith answered the door. Red was left speechless. When Faith opened the door, her robe opened and exposed her breast, as she had planned, but pretended not to know. Red couldn't help but look and lust over them. She saw the look on Red's face and laughed secretly. "Oh! Excuse me!" she said trying to act innocent. "I was about to get into the shower when I heard the doorbell ring. What brings you here, Red?"

"Well, I heard about Twurk's incident and since I saw the Navi, I thought they were all here. I'm sorry for disturbing you," said Red. "Well, they were here, but they had some business to go handle. You know how y'all do!" she said as she smiled and flashed a nipple. "Well, just tell them I stopped by!" said Red with a devilish grin on his face. "Tell them to call me too," he said looking dead at Faith and all her glory. He was just about to say something else when Faith closed the door. He didn't want to knock on the door again because that would be too obvious so he just left. As he left he touched the Navi and prayed to himself for Twurk to not give up but keep fighting to get better. Thang watching from the window thought it looked creepy and felt like Red was acting as if Twurk died. "His creepy ass! My brother ain't dead! He lucky I ain't smoke his ass from trying to hustle us at the courts. If it wasn't for Twurk, he would be!" he thought to himself.

Faith entered the room. "Thang, I think he might suspect something. The way he looked at me kind of gave me the creeps!" she said sounding a bit nervous. Thang stared out the window as Red drove away with a million and one thoughts running through his mind. Faith crept up behind him and pressed her breasts up against his back as she reached around to rub his chest. He turned around and she pressed her body against his and slowly slid down until her mouth met his manhood all while staring him in the eyes. "Now, where were we?" she said with a smile as she took him into her mouth.

Five is on the highway and is headed home after picking up a ring, flowers, and chocolates as a surprise for Faith. He is vibin' along to the love songs on the radio thinking of the two of them together forever. He almost couldn't believe he is ready to turn in his player card to settle down with just one woman.

Faith was on the bed with her face buried in the pillow while Thang was pounding her from behind doggy style. He pulled her hair to raise her up and started tongue kissing her aggressively. This was what she had been craving from Thang all alone. Only he knew how to truly satisfy her inner freak. "Look at us!" he told her. "Look in the mirror! Is this the future you want?" "Yes!" she replied looking at how her body shook with each thrust. "Can he fuck you like me? Can he make that pussy come like me?" he asked her while getting more aggressive. Her moans only seem to motivate him to go harder. She loved every minute of the pleasure and the pain. After she orgasmed she just collapsed onto the bed as he marveled over his work with a gloating smile. He leaned down and have her a kiss on the cheek. "I'll be back in due time!" he said as he slapped her on the ass. He got dressed then left her there in the fetal position still moaning from the pleasure.

Thang hit the highway and lit up a blunt and took a sip from a mini bottle of Red Passion. He thought about how blind Five is when it comes to women, especially Faith and why of all the women in the world, he wanted to marry her.

Five finally made it home. He opened the door and made his way to the bedroom where he thought Faith would be. He opened the bed room door and made his way over to Faith who was now pretending to be sleep. She had just finished creating a scene of soft music, scented candles, and rose petals to cover up the prior one that took place before Five arrived. She got back into bed as he pulled into the drive way. "Baby, are you awake? Daddy's home! I have a surprise for you!" he said as he kissed her on her cheek. "Hmm! Is that you book?" she asked as she slowly opened her eyes. He opened the small box to display a diamond filled ring.

Chapter 9

Peaches sat alone in her room on her bed trying to relax and rid herself of the tension and guilt she had been carrying since the incident with Twurk. She was wondering if he was okay or had he been killed. She fell back onto the soft pillow watching the ceiling fan blades spin around until her eyelids became heavy and her eyes closed.

Downstairs. Strawberry and Choc were washing dishes. Strawberry was jamming to the radio when Choc touched her arm to get her attention. She turned towards her to see she had a serious look on her face. "What?" Strawberry asked Choc. "We need to find out what has been bothering Peaches? Can't you tell something is up with her or have you not noticed?" she said as she snatched Strawberry's headset away from her ear. "You can be an ass sometimes! I just want to you to know that!" she added as she stormed off out the kitchen. "Whatever!" yelled Strawberry as she put back on her headset and continued to wash dishes.

Thang, was still thinking about the words Faith spoke to him earlier about Red suspecting something. He was starting to feel the change in himself and life in general being that Twurk was in the hospital. He now felt somewhat removed from his brother's shadow. He had always been the loose cannon of the two and Twurk was more stable. He took a pull from the blunt before exiting the Navi and into the "Taste-n-Mix" store.

Pink pulled into the parking lot of 'Taste-n-Mix'. She glanced over at Thang's Navi and thought it looked somewhat familiar. "I wonder if that is ole boy?" she thought to herself. She looked back at her girls who were jamming to a song on the stereo by Lil Kim and laughed before she asked them if they were thirsty. "Hell yeah!" they replied and they all got out of the car.

Thang had made his way down the candy aisle. His sweet tooth was kicking in since he had been drinking and smoking all day. He grabbed a pack of mango-flavored bubble gum and threw one in his mouth as his eyes spotted two red bones at the end of the aisle. "Damn, now that's some eye candy!" he said under his breath.

Strawberry and Choc were on the chip aisle opening their favorite bags. They started eating and throwing chips at each other playfully. Peaches stood still when she saw what they were doing. She couldn't help but laugh along. "Pink is going to have a fit! I want no parts of this!" and she turned to leave. Suddenly, she felt a chip hit her back. She paused, and faced them both. "Oh hell no!" she said as she grabbed a bag of chips to get them back. Pink walked up on the aisle they were on to see her girls acting a fool and chips all over the floor. "Y'all better---!" Before she could say anything else she was hit by a chip then couldn't help but giggle and shake her head slowly at how juvenile they were but also happy in that moment.

Thang walked up on the two red bones he spotted earlier by the counter trying to charm the man behind the counter. They turned around just as he was walking up and immediately started screaming while bouncing up and down, making sure their cleavage was doing the same. They recognized him from the performance he and Twurk did at the Playas & Ballers. Thang tried to play it cool. He licked his lips and approached them. "What's happening ladies?" he said with a smile. "We recognize you from Playas & Ballers" said the tallest one. "You and your twin shut it down!" she added as she dropped it low to the ground and wound it back up slow. Thang started undressing them with his eyes. He was loving the attention. "Can we get an autograph?" said the tall one. "Can we get a picture?" said the short one. "Sure!" said Thang. They sandwiched Thang in between the two of them and snapped the photo with their cameras. After they took the photo they were still stuck on Thang's sides smiling in a flirtatious manner as he smiled back.

Pink and her girls walked up on them checking out what was going on. "Can I help you young ladies with anything else?" asked Thang as he saw Pink and her friends walking in their direction. The two girls looked at each other and gave a head nod. They turned back towards Thang then lifted up their shirts. "We want your autograph, right here!" said the tall one as they jiggled their breasts about. Thang was all too happy to oblige as he asked for a marker from the guy behind the counter.

"Hello!" said Pink fed up from the groupie actions. "If you and your fans are done here, me and my girls would like to check out, if it's not too much to ask?" Thang looked Pink up and down and looked at the rest of the crew. He recognized Strawberry right away. "Of course! Anything for the ladies!" he said to Pink. He went to the counter to pay for his purchases and gave the man a crisp one-hundred-dollar bill. "Take care of the ladies! Keep the change!" he said. He gave Strawberry a wink and flashed Pink a smile before he walked out of the door.

Pink requested four drinks from the cashier and was about to pay for all their items, when the guy told her that it was already paid for. "What?!" said Pink. "The guy in front of you, he paid for everyone!" he told Pink. She turned to look at her girls then in the direction Thang departed to, but he was already gone.

Pink and her girls got in the ride and got back on the highway. Along the drive, Pink was trying to figure out why Thang paid for their purchases. Typically, when a man does that, it has always been some part of the game in her experience with men. She was trying to figure what would be his motive being that he's never had conversation with any of them. The thoughts were distracting her focus on the road until Strawberry hit her with an elbow to the arm. "Damn! Where are you? Focus on the road! You are driving, you know?" she told Pink. "You almost zoomed past that unmarked car over there. We don't need those type of problems!" she added. "I saw that car!" said Pink trying to play it off. She eased off the gas and made sure to keep her focus.

Thang called his mom after leaving the store. As soon as his mom answered the phone he said, "Mom! Anything on Twurk? Did the doctor call? Any news?" bombarding her with questions. "Hello Mom! How are you doing mom? Those things would be a more proper greeting, but no there has not been any new updates," she replied to Thang. "You can call for yourself, son! I love you!" she said before ending the call. Thang sat at the stop light and to his left a flyer caught his eye. It mentioned the "Rep Yo Ride" contest which was a car and bike show. The flyer mentioned good food, performing artists and Thang's favorite type of contest, the wet t-shirt contest. He and Twurk would definitely be in the spot if Twurk were there with him. So, he decided he was going for him and for Twurk. He turned left to head to the contest instead of the right to go back home.

P-Murder and his crew were out joyriding and taking a break from working over the two ballers for the day. They ended up the mix of people traveling towards the "Rep Yo Ride" event. At first the slow traffic, was getting him agitated, but thinking about the big payoff he felt was coming calmed him. Especially, since he would be able to floss in a ride as nice as the ones he saw going towards the event. To check out the future competition, he decided they would follow the rest of the crowd to the contest.

Pink and her girls were shopping at the mall to get some retail therapy at some baller's expense. They were in line to pay for their purchases when they were behind some females talking to the cashier about the "Rep Yo Ride" contest that was happening today. "Girl, that motherfucker is going to be jumpin'! Everybody from all over is going to be out there! The "Rep Yo Ride" contest is what's poppin'! I wish you could go, but you gotta work! I'll take some pictures for you though!" said the girl at the counter as she laughed. Pink and the girls were serviced by another cashier in the store but finished their purchase the same time as the girl having a conversation with the cashier. They picked up their bags to leave the store when they were stopped by the cashier that was speaking to the other customer. "Hey! Are y'all going to the contest too?" she asked. To which Strawberry replied, "Where do we find this contest at?" "Oh! It's over on B street by the strip. Over near Craig's spot! Everybody knows Craig with his fine ass! Speaking of Craig's fine ass, I just want to fu--" "Thank you!" said Strawberry cutting off the cashier mid-sentence and leaving her a bit stunned. They leave the store with a good laugh and a new destination.

"It's jumping like a motherfucker out here!" said Jitty as he took in all the crowds of people who were at the event and the ones that were still coming in. "You damn right! I ain't never seen this much pussy in one spot! Look at shawty in the purple thong! She got ass for days. I feel like a shark in a sea of fish!" said Reaper. "Yeah! This might turn out just fine. I see a bunch of ducks in the water to hunt!" said P-Murder.

Heat just continued to smoke his blunt not paying any mind to what the others were talking about. All that was on his mind was the many different ways he could kill Peaches. He just couldn't let it go. He smiled inside at the delight of being able to carry it out.

At the entrance, Pink and her girls were looking for a parking spot so they can join the festivities. They lucked up and found one close to main entrance as a car pulled out from the spot. "Now this is what I'm talking about! Fun time, baby!" said Strawberry with a big koolaid smile as she watched the action going on around her. She got so excited that she started bouncing around in her seat. "Damn right! It's on and poppin' out here! I don't know about y'all but I need me a drink!" said Choc as she watched people walk by with their beverages. Pink, who saw that Peaches was not in tuned with the rest of them as she looked out the window, put her hand on her knee and gave her a smile. "Peaches, I know you ain't gonna miss out on all this fun? Put a smile on your face and cheer up!" she said as she grabbed Peaches' face playfully. Peaches, wanting to be able to have fun with her girls gave in. "Yea we did come to have fun so who am I to stop the party! Let's go have fun and maybe get a little wet in this wet t-shirt contest!" she said as she pointed towards the sign for the contest. Peaches and Pink exchanged glances that said everything they didn't say out loud as Pink knew Peaches was still having a hard time and only wanted her girl to stay strong because she as usual had her back. They all went to the wet t-shirt contest booth to sign up. Afterwards, they went to get drinks.

Thang finally made his way to the "Rep Yo Ride" contest. He had his music blasting so loud as if he was trying to get the "best booming system" award. Others turned to look as he pulled into the spot and parked. He looked around to see what the crowd looked like. As he looked closer to the main entrance he saw Pink's Lexus. "Damn! This must be my lucky day, twice in one day!" He just sat in his ride with his .45 in his lap and lit up a blunt as he watched the ongoing activity around him.

Being already alerted of Thang's presence due to his music, Roc told P-Murder, "Look! There goes ole "Green Eyes"! Want me to do the honors?" as he brandished his piece. "Nah, this ain't the time nor the place," P-Murder replied. Suddenly a voice, came over the loud speaker. "Ladies and gentlemen, I'm Craig, the host for today's "Rep Yo Ride" event. It's about that time fellas! Ladies, it's time to get wet!" he said signaling the contestants to get ready for the wet t-shirt contest. The men in the crowd were going wild at this point which caused P-murder and his crew to look towards the stage.
"What the fuck?!" said Heat, stunned as he saw Peaches enter the stage. The rage came back all over again.

Thang, on the other hand, took pleasure in watching the girls entertain the crowd. His manhood's erection was a sure reflection of how much he liked what he saw. "That's what I'm talking about! Showtime!" he thought to himself as he took a pull from the blunt.

Pink and the crew was loving the crowd watching them and started to stare down the competition who was already staring back at them for trying to steal the show. A total of eight were to compete in this competition, but in groups of four. The other group of four called themselves P.H.A.T. (Pretty Hot and Tempting). They were all dressed in the white T-shirts swimming shorts provided by the event hosts. The crowd cheered as the ones down front readied their big super soaker guns. "DJ! Let's get that theme music going!" said Craig signaling the start of the show. The deejay started to play French Montana's song, "Work" which got the crowd crunk. Then the first blasts of water started to come and Strawberry was up first. The rest of the crew started to dance and twerk for the audience around her.

"Damn! Them bitches up there are workin'! That chick with the pink hair! Strawberry! She got it going on!" Jitty told Reaper. "Fool, you don't have to tell me! Ain't no way I can forget all that ass on Choc. You can sit a tray of bottles on that thang! This is like a real live version of "Girls Gone Wild" but better! Just look at all that ass shaking going on up there!" said Reaper.

Craig reappeared on stage after all the water had stopped flowing. He walked around the group of ladies staring them down from head to toe as he shook his head and licked his lips in a playboy type of way. "Ooo wee! Fellas, this is definitely going to be a hard one and I do mean a "hard one"! Alright! Alright y'all! It's time to pick a winner!" he said as he walked back and forth between the groups of ladies. "Can we get the noise-o-meter out here please?" he said to the stage hand. "Alright let's hear it for P.H.A.T.!" The crowd went wild enough to bring the meter up to a reading of 7. "Alright let's hear it for Pink & her crew!" The crowd sent the meter all the way to 10 making Pink and her crew the clear winners. As a thank you, they put on a little extra show for the crowd grinding, twerking and grabbing each other's tits. Some people in the crowd started to throw money on the stage. Strawberry and Choc shared a sexy and erotic kiss that sent the crowd into a frenzy and resulted in even more money being thrown on the stage. They giggled at the melee they were causing but thanked the people for the win and the funds. Pink was finally happy to see Peaches happy and smiling along with the rest of the girls like old times.

"Y'all definitely put on a show today!" said Craig. "We always try to give the crowd their money's worth!" said Strawberry as she gave the crowd a final twerk, then ended with a split. "Damn!" said Craig. "Let's hear it one more time for Pink and the crew!"

The crowd showed their appreciation. Craig and the other event workers gave them their prize trophy and prize money. They each got $500 a piece. "Damn! If I knew it was gon' be that easy, we would have been coming here more often!" said Pink to her girls. "You got that right! Like Future say—Free Bandz!" added Strawberry putting an extra wiggle in her walk. They left the stage to get dress and then headed back to their car. "I think we need to hit up the club tonight!" said Pink. "I'm all in!" said Strawberry now looking at Peaches and Choc who seemed to be in agreement. Pink turned up the music as they got in the car. They were jamming all the way until they got out of the parking lot.

Thang had been watching Strawberry with every move she made all the way to their car until they pulled out the parking lot. He was determined to one day "show her what a real man felt like". He said to himself that he would have to hit up social media to see if they can connect. Now that the fun was over, he felt it was time for him to leave too. As he crunk up the car, his phone rung. He looked at the phone and realized it was the girls he met earlier today. "Yo! What is on your mind, shawty?" he said as he answered the phone. "Me and my girl are trying to get up with you? What's it going to be, big daddy?" said the voice on the other end. "Oh, for real? Shoot me the location and give me about an hour! One!" he said as he hung up the phone. Thang smiled as he thought about the many positions he had planned for them. He put the location into his GPS and headed there.

"Yo Heat! What's up with you? You've been quiet all day! Anybody you need me to get for you?" asked Roc. "I'm straight, man! Just in my zone that's all!" Heat told Roc. P-Murder looked at the two of them and even though Heat told Roc that he was fine, P-Murder knew what was going on with him and what he planned on doing. He was a hard-head and a hot head. The situation could very well be a volatile one for the rest of the crew if he moves without thinking.

Thang had finally made it to his destination and anticipated fulfilling every desire the two red bones could think of as well as his own. He scoped the scenery around him because he'd never been there before and wasn't about to be caught slippin' anywhere. He was about to cut the car off and get out when he got a text alert on his phone. He recognized the number so he opened the message to find it was from the doctor. After reading the message, he whipped the Navi around so fast he barely missed a mailbox. He took off in the direction of the hospital.

Chapter 10

"Hey boo!" I tried to stay awake for you. I just--" said Faith as she was silenced by Five's finger on her lips. "Shh! It's okay baby, you don't have to explain. Right now, I just want to please you. You are my everything and everything deserves to be yours!" he said as he sat down on the bed next to her while staring into her eyes. He had the ring box in his hand prepared to pop the question. Faith, in anticipation for what's about to happen next, maneuvered herself in the bed to sit upright with the covers draping over her as to show a little cleavage and her bare sides. Five, realizing that Faith was naked, thought this created the perfect setting for him to pop the question. "Faith! Will you marry me?"

Faith's whole world came to a pause. Many thoughts came to her mind at once. She knew in her heart she is in love with Five because of all he has done for her and the money he has makes her love him even more and to let all that go would make her a fool. However, her body and a piece of her heart longs for Thang because he satisfies her sexually. She craved him when they are apart for long periods of time. She hoped that Thang comes up with a plan to put in motion before everything is jeopardized by Red who may put the pieces together and tells Five what he suspects. She had it in her mind that before she lets anyone ruin anything for her, she will handle business herself.

Meanwhile, Five was cringing on the inside as he kept looking at Faith waiting for an answer. He hoped she wouldn't say no because it would be detrimental to their bond as well as their relationship. He almost let his head drop, when Faith blurted out, "Yes! I will marry you!" Tears formed in the corners of her eyes but not because of the proposal. Five was so excited by her response. He placed the ring on her finger and moved her other hand, allowing the covers to fall revealing her naked body. He leaned in to her and started caressing her breasts passionately while kissing her.

After making it home, Pink and her girls settled in. Peaches finished showering and went to her room to dry her hair. She sat in front of her mirror and looked at all of the old pictures of her and her girls when they were wild and free. She started reminiscing and fell into a trance. She went from seeing her and her girls in her mind to seeing Twurk. He was standing next to some chick dressed in wedding attire. The preacher standing between the two of them announced them husband and wife. The once happy smiling faces in the crowd turned to the evil grins of demons. As he went to pull the bride close to him for a kiss, he was snatched away from the bride by the preacher who now appears to be the devil. Twurk tried to free himself from the preacher's grip to reach his bride who was taken by the demons from the crowd. They devil threw Twurk to the demons and they started ripping him to shreds. "Peaches!" Twurk screamed out. "You two souls are mine!" said the devil as he turned and pointed at Peaches. The bride reappeared from amongst the demons and lifted her veil to reveal that she was a demon as well. This woke Peaches from her trance. She was almost out of breath and tried to calm herself. "That was weird as hell!" she said. She went to her closet to look for an outfit trying to put the imagery out of her mind.

Pink finished getting dressed and thought back over the events of the day from Thang's little performance at the Taste-n-Mix, the shopping and the wet t-shirt contest. She felt she really had a great day with her girls. As she started to leave the room, her phone rung. She quickly grabbed the phone from her dresser and saw that it was an unknown number. "Hello! Who are you and how did you get my number?" is how she answered. "This is Five!" said the voice on the other line. "I got your number from a friend of mine. I hope I'm not interrupting anything but I got a little gig coming up! Could you and your girls come put on a show tonight?" he asked Pink. "Long as you got the bread, we'll be there!" she said. "Alright, I'll send you the details," said Five before ending the call.

Peaches heard a bump against her window. She peered from the closet to see a little hummingbird on her window sill. She opened the window to try to help the injured bird. She reached for the bird carefully but then a knock at the door startled her so she accidentally dropped the bird. It didn't fully hit the ground before it got scooped up by a tom cat. Peaches stood there gasping at what just happened. Strawberry stood outside of Peaches' door knocking but didn't get an answer. "Peaches! Are you alive in there?" Strawberry yelled as she opened the door to enter the room. Peaches gave Strawberry a look that made Strawberry think she interrupted something. "Should I come back later?" asked Strawberry. Peaches regaining her composure motioned her to come on in. "What's on your mind, Strawberry?" she asked. "You've got that look in your eye. I can tell something is bothering you. Spill it!" she insisted as she sat down on the bed and motioned for Strawberry to sit too. Strawberry was somewhat hesitant to say what was going on tried to stall by picking up pictures and talking about old times. Peaches took Strawberry's hands and looked her in the eyes and told her that whatever she was going through that she has her back.

Strawberry inhaled deeply then exhaled. "Peaches! I've been asked out on a date by that guy from the Taste-n-Mix, Thang! He hit me up on social media and said he'd been trying to catch up with me for a while. I love Choc, but something in me wants him so bad ever since I saw him at the courts. I don't want to hurt Choc though! What should I do?" Peaches, felt the heaviness of Strawberry's dilemma. She told her, "You've got to follow your heart to find out who you truly love!" She gave her a hug and sent her on her way. Strawberry left Peaches' room and headed down the hall. As she stood in the doorway of her and Choc's room she replayed the words of advice from Peaches in her mind. She watched Choc lie across the bed in a black thong and matching bra. Her ass was definitely swallowing it whole. She reflected on when they first got together and the times they shared together. "Damn! Where are you Strawberry?" asked Choc breaking up her daydreams. "Didn't you hear me calling you? Peaches must have really dropped the bomb on you to have you in deep thought! Come on over here and let me ease your mind!" said Choc as she licked her lips with strong desire in her eyes. Strawberry smiled and began to walk towards the bed with a smile on her face. Just as she reached the bed, they heard Pink

yell, "Hey, girls! I need y'all at the table! Now!" "Damn!" they
said in unison. They were well familiar with that phrase and
Pink's tone as it usually involved making some money. "Girl,
let's get downstairs!" said Strawberry to Choc.

Pink sat down with all the girls at the table. "Listen up ladies!
We have been asked to strip tonight!" she said. "Girl, are you
serious? For who? And where at?" asked Strawberry exchanging
glances with the rest of the girls as they giggled. "Five, from
Playas & Ballers, called me. They want us to put on a show
tonight. Are y'all down or not?" she asked. They looked at one
another. "We're in!" they said in unison. "Let's get this money!"
said Pink and then they all departed from the table.

Back at P-Murder's crib, they were sitting around lounging.
"Jitty, you always gotta be the comedian, and your jokes ain't
funny! Now that breath of yours, that's some funny shit!" said
Roc as he and everyone else laughed. "Man, I know you ain't
talking! Soon as you opened your mouth I saw thirty flies enter
the room!" he barked back. "Y'all that contest was off the chain,
wasn't it? Them hoes were so damn fine, I could barely focus!"
said Jitty. "I'm willing to bet if I wanted to catch Jitty, all I
would have to do is send some bad broads in and wait for a little
bit. Then I'd walk in and catch him slippin'! Bam!" said Reaper
as the rest of the gang laughed. "Fuck all that! Are we gonna hit
Playas & Ballers tonight is all I wanna know?" asked P-Murder.
"There is going to be a strip show poppin' off. I'm talking bad ass
hoes galore!" he said with a smirk on his face.

At the hospital, Thang entered the elevator and pressed the
button for the fifth floor. Flashes of the moments he just shared
with Faith ran through his mind. His thought process was
interrupted by the ding of the elevator. The door opened and he
got off on the floor and headed toward Twurk's room. When he
got to the door he saw Twurk and the doctor casually talking to
each other. He walked inside. "What's good bro?" said Twurk as
Thang walked in the room. "What it do, bro? What's good, doc?"

asked Thang as he dapped up Twurk and shook the doctor's hand.

"Hey doc? I'm still free to leave, right? Cause I've been in this bed for too damn long!" said Twurk. "Yeah! You and your brother are free to "ball til you fall" as you put it!" he said as they all laughed. "Doc, what you know about ballin'?" asked Thang. "Somebody's been learning a little something in here!" Thang said jokingly. "Thanks for all you've done for my family and specifically for me," added Twurk. "You're quite welcome!" said the doctor. As they left, the hospital and exited the double doors, Twurk finally caught a glimpse of fresh air. When they made it to the Navi, Twurk stood still staring at the Navi's still impressive paint work. Thoughts of his father and their conversations ran through his until he was hit in the chest with a set of keys which he caught in his hand due to reflex. He then looked at his brother. "What?" he said surprised at Thang giving him the keys. "Shit! Don't look all surprised! You're driving like always so let's go!" Thang told Twurk as he giggled. They both got inside. Twurk adjusted the mirrors and seat to his former settings. Thang was checking out Twurk getting back into the swing of things. "You need to put this baby in the wind! So that you can go clean up and start looking like Twurk again," said Thang as he lit up a blunt. Twurk crank up the car determined to push through the remaining jitters he may have and remembering the words his father spoke to him while unconscious. He looked over at Thang, who was clearly in relax mode. "Man! Pass the blunt! Twurk's back!" he told his brother as he held out his hand to receive the blunt from Thang. They left the parking lot to head home. Thang received a text from Five, to let him know a party was going on tonight. He texted him back and told him Twurk was out of the hospital. Five insisted that Thang bring Twurk along as well to celebrate his homecoming. Thang told Twurk about the party and how Five really wants him to come, but insisted Twurk be the one to break to their mom since he will have more favor.

On the other side of town, Pile-Up is driving around and making sure his soldiers are working overtime to find the yellow

Hummer and all its inhabitants to reconcile what has happened to two of their own. Money was in the backseat overseeing the progress as the reports were coming in and hitting a line or two in the process. They pulled up on one of their lil' soldiers who told them that the word was that they could possibly be at the event that was happening at Playas and Ballers tonight and they will put the word out to keep an eye out for the Hummer and P-Murder and his crew. Pile-Up pulled out ten crispy hundred-dollar bills and handed it to the boy. "You be good mon!" he said as he pulled off.

Five poured two glasses of red passion and handed one of them to Faith. "Baby, I am so glad to have you attending the party tonight! I love you so much! You are my everything! To us, forever!" he said to Faith as he raised his glass for a toast. She raised her glass to meet his and he pulled her close by grabbing her ass and then passionately kissed her on the neck. "Anything for you babe!" said Faith. She didn't mind letting Five feel like a king but deep within she longed for Thang to quench the fire that burned within. She could feel the juices trickle down her inner thigh in anticipation.

Twurk and Thang finally made it home and pulled into their driveway. The two watched their mom, who was sitting on the porch waiting for them, stand up and come down to greet them. She was excited to see her baby boys together again. She came running towards Twurk as he got out with open arms. "Baby! I'm so glad to have you back! Please don't take me through this again!" she said pleading with him. "Damn! I love you too mom!" said Thang jealous at all the love Twurk was getting. "I'm going to go hit the showers if anybody needs me!" he said jokingly as he shook his head and went into the house.

"Don't worry about Thang! That is his way of expressing his love! He don't really mean any harm. You know how he gets. Mom, I am back now and I'm not leaving you again. I had plenty of conversations with dad while I was in the hospital. He said to tell you that he loved you and for me to take care of you guys. He's watching over all of us, mom!" A tear rolled down his mom's face before she wiped it away and composed herself.

"Let's go inside!" she said as they locked arms to walk towards the door. As they enter the house they are met by Thang who had stopped to grab a snack and secretly peer at them from the living room window. "Dang, y'all acting like lovers or something! Get a room already!" he said as he laughed. It was his defense from feeling any real emotion and they knew. They laughed as well as he went to take his shower.

Thang let the hot water run down his body as he thought about all the women he has been with and Faith came to mind as the frontrunner. "Damn! She must have me pussy whipped!" he thought to himself and insisting that he definitely had to shake that off. Then he remembered that Faith also told him that she thought Red suspected the two of them were messing around, which made him more alert in the presence and less concerned about the sea of women he had swam in.

Twurk and mom continued to sit and talk together as Twurk buttered her up for what he was about to tell her. "Sooo...mom, Thang and I were going to attend this party tonight. Five is throwing it. It's like a welcome back celebration for me. You do remember Five, don't you, mom?" asked Twurk. She continued holding on to Twurk's hands while shaking her head in disbelief. "Twurk! You just got back from the hospital and now you are trying to get right back out there to the same ole club?!" she said trying to hold back the tears. Twurk felt the concern his mother had and saw the grief all over her face. He gave her a hug and kissed her on the forehead. "Mom! Don't worry! Thang and I will be safe, okay!" he told his mom as he flashed her a charming smile. "I'm going to hit the shower. I love you mom!" he told her as he left the room. She watched as he walked away. "Yeah! That's what you said the last time before you got shot!" she thought to herself as she wiped away a single tear.

Twurk was anxious to take a shower and wash the hospital juju off him. He stood underneath the showerhead to let the hot water relieve the tension in his muscles that were sore from being laid up in the hospital bed and the rest of his body was still sore from surgery. Twurk closed his eyes and drifted away. He found himself in the middle of nowhere in the woods. A female voice called out to him saying that something was wrong. "Where are you? I can hear you but I can't see you! I'm here!" he yelled out towards the voice. He began to make his way through the woods following the voice and getting closer. Once near the voice, he comes face to face with a gigantic black widow spider. "Twurk, help me!" yelled out the voice again. "I'm coming!" he yelled back. He looked around to find a sturdy tree limb then swung at the spider. He missed but the mere attempt sent the spider back up into its web. He used the stick to beat some of the web out of the pathway to get to where the voice was coming from. He looked in the distance to see the female running towards him from a headless horseman with a sword in hand. He ran to try to save her jumping over fallen trees along the way. The distance between the woman and the horseman getting shorter and shorter until the woman realized her fate was   sealed. She looked at Twurk, who was running in her direction, with tears streaming down her face. Suddenly, with a swipe of his sword, he took her head clean off. Twurk stopped in his tracks realizing what had just happened. The horseman jumped off the horse to retrieve the head and then threw it at Twurk. He returned to his horse then produced a head to place on his torso. The face was shockingly familiar with a pair of evil green eyes that pierced his soul.

He is disturbed by a knock at the door that brought him back to the present. "Man are you alright in there?" asked Thang. He was a bit disturbed by the vision he just had but tried to shake it off. He didn't realize how long he had been in the shower. "Are you bathing like a girl or showering man?" asked Thang jokingly. "Give me a few, bro!" he told Thang as he continued showering. The hot water was starting to wane so it wouldn't be long.

Later, Twurk resurfaced into the living room Thang stood up ready to go as he told the person on the phone they'd be on their way soon. "Damn! I thought you were drowning in the tub! Glad to see you're back because you were looking like hell earlier!" said Thang jokingly as mom punched him in the arm. "What?!"

he said to mom as they both laughed. "You know your brother just got out of the hospital! Don't be so insensitive!" she told Thang. Thang smiled and kissed his mom on the cheek. "Ok mom! I love you but don't wait up! We will be alright tonight! Twurk I'll be in the Navi!" he said as he walked out the door. Mom now stood looking directly at Twurk. She folded her arms as a means of protest but he eventually won her over by flashing her a smile that melted her a little. "Son! Please just come back safe, okay?" she said as she held his hands and dropped her head. He sensed her frustration and her pain. He grabbed her by the chin and raised her head while giving her a smile. "Mom, don't worry. Please just get some sleep tonight! I love you!" he said as he kissed her on her forehead and then gave her a big hug before walking out the door.

Thang looked Twurk over as he got inside the ride. "It's good to have you back bro!" he told him.

Chapter 11

At club "Playas & Ballers", everything was going exactly as Five planned for them to go. "Red, I'm so glad that you could make it tonight!" He passed Red a glass of Red Passion and they toasted to the night before taking a sip. They both watched the crowd below while it continued to grow as more and more people showed up. Red thought about mentioning his suspicions about Faith being scandalous and that he might not be able to trust Thang, but he realized how much he was into her and the news might crush him. "I wouldn't miss this night for the world!" he told Five. "Not even at the risk of getting chewed out by my ole lady and you know how she can get!" he added. He took another sip of his drink.

Pink and her crew arrived at the club. They gave themselves a quick inspection before heading to the door. At the entrance, they were met by two bouncers. "Pink and the crew?" one of the bouncers asked. "Yes, that's us! We are here pretty boy!" she said flirtatiously. "I'm Trey and this is Dave. He will show you to your V.I.P. room," he said. They followed him into the club and into the V.I.P. that was meant for them. Peaches admired the beautiful décor in the room. "Wow!" This is very nice and cozy. I can get used to this kind of treatment! This carpet makes me feel like I am walking on clouds but God knows I am far from an angel" she said as they all laughed. "Well, while we are here, let's make the most of our stay!" said Pink to her girls as she popped the cork off the first bottle of Moet.

P-Murder and his crew arrived shortly thereafter. They sat in the Hummer watching all the people go in. "Let's hope no one recognizes us from the last time!" said P-Murder looking dead at Heat. "Let's go!" he said. They all got out and made their way into the club. They went to the back to sit as usual and ordered bottles of Cristal. "I gotta to give it to the owner of this club, he got taste and he keep a packed house," said Jitty. Roc was scoping the crowd.

Twurk and Thang pulled into the club parking spot with the music blasting loud and smoking on blunts as usual. They entered the club through the secret entrance that lead them to an elevator which takes them directly to the sky box. They knew Five would be there. On the elevator ride up, Thang looked over to Twurk sensing that he was a little distant. "Twurk, I got the feeling that tonight is going to be a good night! What about you, bro?" "You already know bruh! Regardless of what we go through or what happens to us along the way, we are always gonna be the best! Even when we are gone. They will never make or find another pair like Twurk & Thang!" replied Twurk. The elevator doors opened and they proceeded to the skybox.

Twurk and Thang entered the skybox where they were greeted by Red sipping on their signature drink, Red Passion. On the other side of the room, Five stood with Faith by his side wearing a skin tight crème colored dress. She smiled at the both of them but gave Thang a look of lust and desire when others weren't paying attention. Five came up to Twurk to give him a hug after he had finished dapping up Red. "I'm glad you too were able to make it, especially you Twurk. Tonight, is all about you! It is good to have you back! Red, hook them up with some glasses of Red Passion!" said Five. Red gave them both a glass and raised his glass to toast to Twurk and his recovery.

"So, you gonna act like you don't see me, Twurk?" I know they are your bros and all but don't forget about your sis!" said Faith. "Come and give me some love! You are still looking as handsome as ever!" she said as she embraced him and placed a kiss on his cheek then quickly wiped away the lipstick print. "Damn! How long have I been gone? Am I seeing correctly? Is this an engagement ring?" he asked seeing the many diamonds blinging on Faith's ring finger. Thang and Red who were engaged in conversation, stopped talking and turned their heads to see the ring in which Twurk was talking about and see Five and Faith both showing the ring to Twurk. Thang looked at Faith who was staring at him through a side eye but also basking in the moment taking place.

"Hey, Twurk! I know you just got out of the hospital and all, but I was just wondering if you and your brother would give us a little performance tonight? You know, for old time sake. Show them that y'all still got it!" pleaded Five. Twurk, looked at Five, but thought about it for a moment being all that he had just went through. However, on the strength of their relationship and Five's loyalty, he thought it only a small request and he should
honor it. "Don't nobody rock the stage like y'all! Y'all were born to do music! I ain't going to say too much because I don't want to stroke your ego, but hands down, y'all are the best to ever come through here. One day, I will be telling people that I grew up with y'all two legends. The inseparable Twurk & Thang!" added Red.

Faith with her hands now wrapped around Five's waist chimed in on the conversation. "Y'all don't want to let your fans down, do you? They have been waiting for your return. Everybody has been trying to take the spotlight, but what has been predestined, no one can stop. Y'all know what the people want, so go and quench their thirst!" she said to them before taking a sip of her drink. She made sure to look Thang right in the eye then look down at his mid-section to let him know she wasn't just talking about a musical performance. Red caught the interaction between Faith and Thang. He blinked twice hoping he didn't just see what he saw. He went to pour himself another drink as not saying anything to Five was eating him up inside.

Thang on the other hand, was even more turned on at the potential danger in their affair. It was like a game of Russian Roulette to him with adrenaline pumping to the head above and below. He gave a smirk. "Well I'm quite sure we will up for any performance tonight, right bro?" he assured them and especially Faith who smirked as well while sipping her drink. Twurk, did a recap of all the faces and finally gave in. "Let's get it bro!" he said to Thang.

Pink and her girls were relaxed and feeling kind of toasty wearing little to nothing. Then, came a knock at the door. "Come in!" yelled Pink. Trey stuck his head in and said, "It's showtime, ladies! Follow me!" They all left the room behind Trey.

Five appeared on stage. He took the mic and started to do his favorite dance, the stanky leg. He was feeling himself thanks to the alcohol and blunts he had earlier. "What's up y'all? I got some great entertainment for y'all! It's going down in Playas & Ballers tonight! Like this eye candy that's about to hit the stage! I don't know if y'all ready for this! Oooh Lawd! Without further ado, give it up for "Pink & the crew"!" he said. He left the stage as the lights dimmed. The background lights turned Pink and sexy music played as each of them made their way to their positions body rolling and winding along the way. Then the beat dropped to play "Raindrops" by Jeremih and they began the show. The crowd was loving every minute of it. They made use of all the props on stage from the chairs to the confetti, and water bottles. Strawberry made her way to Choc's part of the stage and started dancing with her until she was directly behind her winding and grinding in unison. She grabbed Choc around her waist started gliding her hands up her stomach to her chest. She grabbed and caressed both of Choc's breast and eventually removed her bra, tossing it into the audience which threw them into a frenzy. The response was so loud that it was deafening. Pink, seeing the reaction and love her girls were getting decided to up the ante. She climbed to the top of the pole, removed her bra and slid down the pole but stopping along the way to make her titties bounce for the crowd. She did a flip into and landed in a split before reaching the ground. She crawled away from the pole a bit and starting poppin' and twerking in a doggy-style position to the beat of the song.

Peaches walked over to Pink and smacked her on the booty. Then got in the downward dog postion over Pink and started poppin to the same rhythm. Afterwards, she stood directly behind her and once again smacked her on the booty before relieving Pink of her thong. Pink turned away from the crowd and exposed all her glory as she continued to pop and twerk for them. By the end of the show, the crowd was showering them with so much money that it definitely made the earnings from the wet t-shirt contest look like chump change.

Outside the club, Pile-Up was scanning the parking lot looking for their target. After spotting the yellow Hummer, he decided to park away from their target's site, but in a spot that would give them the vantage point. Money was in the back seat with his black chopper laid next to him. "Me see dey are here! Good!" said Money to Pile-Up before hitting two lines. "Money, do we go in or wait out here?" Pile-Up asked. Money stared at Pile-Up through the rearview mirror while rubbing Killa and Murda on the head. "Let's wait! Me want to catch them off guard. Dat's how dey got me so I'm returning the favor!" he replied.

Inside, after the girl's show had closed, the lights on stage went out again, leaving everyone wondering what's coming up next. Red lights came on in the background, giving the crowd a big clue as to who was next on the stage. Shadows of two figures appeared and then the lights shone finally to reveal Twurk and Thang standing there on stage with their heads down. P-Murder was taken by surprise, starting at Twurk. He looked as if he saw a ghost. "Well! Well! Well! Look at what the wind blew in! Guess this cat must have nine lives or something," thought P-Murder to himself. The rest of the crew noticed the two twins on stage too and was ready for P-Murder to just give the order. However, P-Murder let them know they should just be easy.

As the beat dropped, Twurk came in with "I know it's been a while, but I'm back now, seeing your pretty smile make me change my lifestyle" which was fitting since he had been away for a while and there was obviously something brewing between him and Peaches. The crowd was definitely feeling what he was putting down. Pink and the girls were feeling it too, so much so that they trotted back on stage to dance in front of Twurk and Thang spurring the crowd to make it rain with cash. Thang came in with his verse as it seemed just in line with what was happening. "Shawty ass fat, and I like that. I think I like her style and she give me a chance, I'll make it worth her while," he said eyeing Strawberry. Strawberry seductively strutted over to Thang and started grinding on him. She felt him getting hard which made her get even more hype. Choc caught on to the chemistry. Although she kept on dancing, she was a little hurt inside.

Twurk closed the song with his verse while watching Peaches dance to the beat. He loved the way she moved and wind her hips. After they finished the song, they let the girls have the stage and the deejay kept the music going. They put on one last twerk fest for the crowd. When the song ended, they began to walk and twerk off stage. Strawberry gave Thang a wink on the sly along with a quick glance to his midsection, which he noticed, so he winked back before smacking her on the ass. "I'm about to tap that!" he thought to himself.

Peaches was the last of them in line to leave the stage. She accidentally tripped over the mic cord on her way. Before she could hit the floor, she felt herself being stood back upright. She and Twurk were now face to face and eye to eye. There was so much they wanted to say to each other, but didn't, especially with the visions they have had about each other. "Oh! I feel so-!" started Peaches now red faced. Twurk cuts her off with "-safe, now that we're together?" It wasn't what she was going to say, but he wasn't entirely wrong so she just giggled and blushed even more. "Kind of awkward for us to meet again like this. I do hope we meet again though," he told her. All the while they were still holding on to each other. "Maybe! Time will tell!" said Peaches. "Right now, your fans are calling for an encore," she told him as she freed one of her hands. She gave him a peck on the cheek before freeing the other hand. "Thanks for breaking my fall!" she added as she smiled and jogged away to catch up with the rest of her girls. Twurk couldn't help but stare as she walked away. "What's up bro?" asked Thang breaking Twurk's trance.

"Bro! Trust! I know how you feeling right now? That girl Strawberry got me on fire right now, but we still got a show to do. So, let's focus!" said Thang being the rational one for once. Twurk, recognizing the irony had to laugh, although he knew Thang was telling the truth. They went back on stage to perform another song.

Now back in their room in V.I.P., the girls toasted to the big payoff they just had. "We need gigs like this more often!" said Pink. Strawberry was still crunk from the show but managed to take a moment to chill as she looked at the pile of money in front of them. "I wonder how much money that is on the table! Huh, Choc?" she said. "Why don't you go get green eyes out there? Maybe he can tell you how much it is!" Choc barked back. Everyone in the room went quiet. "Damn! Seems like somebody has an attitude!" said Strawberry trying not to look bothered. Choc turned to Strawberry with fury and said "You damn right I do! You know how I feel when it comes to you! You know I love you and this is what I get in return! Your fucking ass to kiss! He don't love you like I do, he just wants to fuck you! He's a dog just like his brother! They'll fuck you then leave you!"

Peaches looked up in a defensive way because she felt that Twurk had nothing to do with Strawberry and Choc's situation. She started to say something but decided against it. "This is getting too deep for me!" she thought to herself as she took a sip of Moet. A knock on the door broke up the heated argument. In walked Trey, the bouncer that showed them to their room. The tension was so thick he could cut it with a knife so he dared not try to push up on any of them. He handed Pink a yellow envelope. "That came from Five and the family. He has a bachelor party coming soon and would like to know if y'all would be interested in performing?" he asked. "Absolutely!" said Pink speaking on behalf of herself and the girls. "Good! I will relay the message. Y'all were awesome tonight!" he said as flashed them a smile and walked out the door.

Strawberry slid over next to Choc. "Are you still mad at me, boo?" she asked in a sexy and innocent voice that she usually uses to butter up Choc. Choc was not wanting to give in so easily, but once she stared into Strawberry's eyes she couldn't resist. "You know how much I love you, so why are doing this to me? Why, Strawberry? Do I give you any reason to hurt me?" asked Choc as tears ran down her cheeks. Strawberry didn't want to see Choc hurt. She wrapped her arms around her and gave her a kiss on the lips. "I promise, I won't hurt you again! I promise! Now let's count this money, honey!" she told Choc.

They both smiled at the thought of all that cash. Peaches poured her drink after receiving her portion of the money. "Thank God!" she said to herself as the drama had ceased and they were paid.

After killing another performance, Twurk and Thang had made their way back to the elevator to go to the skybox. "Hey bro, we killed it again! Fuck Khaled! We the best!" Thang told Twurk. He was still feeling himself and their performance. "The whole world is going to be requesting us and all the women will be screaming our names, Twurk and Thang! That's all!" replied Twurk. As Twurk and Thang got off the elevator, they were greeted by Red who was all smiles. He congratulated them on a job well done. He opened the door for them as they entered the room and closed the door behind them.

Five was sitting quietly on his all red cushioned fur chair with Faith sitting on the arm. Thang and Twurk got a glass of red passion and sat on the red leather couch across from them. Red was carrying on about how good their performance was until Five cleared his throat to get everyone's attention. "Pardon my interruption!" he said. "I don't mean to cut you off Red, but I must say that you guys are poppin'! You and those four chicks came together to make magic on that stage, naturally! How did y'all do that? Thang I thought you and that chick were about to fuck on the stage the way she was grinding on you!" Faith was not amused as she punched Five in the arm. "My bad boo! Did I go too far?" he asked not knowing it was because she was really jealous of the situation.

Thang, taking the time to stroke his own ego as well as watch Faith squirm did not play down the situation. "Yeah! She surprised me when she pulled that move, but it was a good surprise! She had me ready to go right then and there for a second, then I remembered everyone else was there!" he said as he laughed but also glaring at the expression on Faith's face. She was getting heated but turned on at the same time. Twurk on the other hand, was in a relaxed state and thinking of how Peaches' skin felt against his. Her eyes said so much that she didn't have to say anything. She was like a dream come true. Five noticed how Twurk has went into his own world and laughed to himself as this is how Twurk normally was and it only solidified the fact that he was back to his old self. "Hey Twurk! We are here, man! Where are you?" he laughed. "This is supposed to be your night! Come back with the rest of us, man!" Twurk sat up straight as he focused on all the faces staring back at him. "Damn! I must have kind of drifted off! No disrespect! What did I miss?" he asked as they all laughed.

"So, Twurk, on a more serious note, do you even know who shot you? Cause I'm ready to put holes in whoever fuck with my peoples. Whoever it is, they can get it!" said Five as he raised his shirt to reveal a piece he had tucked away in his waist. Red did a double take when Five revealed the weapon. "Damn Five! Is that thing loaded? Don't scare me like that! Y'all trying to give me a heart attack up in here!" Everyone else in the room giggled as Red was always clowning around. "Seriously though, someone has to answer for fucking with my people and that's on my perm pimpin'!" said Red causing even more laughter.

Twurk enjoyed the funny moments but also took consideration of the sincerity and concern for him from people he called family. "No, I don't know, but when I do find out, it's lights out! That's on my life and not Red's perm!" he said as they all erupted in laughter.

In the parking lot, Money and Pile-Up was still waiting in their spot when Money's phone rung. He answered it reluctantly as he was focused on his target. "Money! I-I need you to over here, now! Poppa is dying! Come now!" said the voice on the other line. "Pile-Up, we go to Haiti! Now! Another time for those fuckers! They best Thank Jah for this moment!" For the first time in a while, Pile-Up saw the fear in Money's eyes. He hit hit the gas pedal and they sped off through the parking lot flying by Pink and her crew who were on their way to their ride.

"Damn! Don't hit me us!" said Pink to the passing vehicle. "This has been a great night! Right, girls?" asked Pink who was tipsy and feeling extra good. "Sure has, girl!" replied Strawberry and Choc as they walked hugged up on one another. Peaches was feeling good, smiling and thinking back on the events of the night. "Twurk seems like an angel that came back just for me," she thought to herself. Pink, observing Peaches' new mood, said, "I'm glad to see you smiling! You must have encountered something you like. As long as you're happy, I'm happy!" she told her. They got in their Lexus and left the club.

Chapter 12

"Believe it or not there hasn't been much action around here lately, since the two ballers got kidnapped and that double homicide that happened. Some people say, the guys that did the kidnapping drive a yellow Hummer, but I haven't heard any names though," said Red. Thang, now intoxicated, looked at Red because he mentioned the murder that claimed Lola's life and because he also thought of the what Faith mentioned to him before. "Five, this has been a great night! I want to thank you for everything!" said Twurk. "Yeah! You're quite welcome! It has been a great night but the most important thing is you're alive and well and you're back with family," said Five sincerely. "Yes, we missed you! It's nice to have you back with us!" added Faith before getting up to whisper something in Fives' ear. She made sure to give Thang a full view of what he's missing. She kissed Five on the cheek and walked seductively as she entered the adjoining room to go to the ladies' room.

"Well, guys it's been a great night and great catching up with you all. Once again, my man Twurk, it's so good to see you alive and back with us bro," said Red as he gave hugs and daps to everyone before leaving. Once he makes it to his car, thoughts of the situation with Faith and Thang play out in his mind. He doesn't like the situation and worst of all, keeping it from Five. He leaves the club parking lot hoping to leave the situation behind for the night.

Up in the skybox, Twurk and Thang were getting ready to leave as well. "Y'all two be safe out there aight!" said Five. "Man, you know we good! Thanks for tonight!" said Thang. "Hey Twurk! Don't scare me like that again man!" added Five jokingly but serious at the same time. "Alright man! As long as time is on my side, I won't!" replied Twurk before closing the door behind him.

Faith came back to find only Five in the room. "Everybody's gone, baby?" asked Faith giving Five the eye. She walked over to him with a 'come-fuck-me" facial expression and lifted him by his collar. She led him over to the couch and pushed him down on it. She straddled him and unbutton his shirt to caress his chest and abs. She unzips his pants to expose his rock-hard manhood. "Looks like somebody is already excited!" she said before she slides down to take him into her wet mouth. "Mmm!" she moaned, causing Five to lean back and relax even more. "That's just what daddy needs!" he tells her as his eyes rolls in the back of his head.

Just before he comes she stops and mounts him in a reverse cowgirl so all he could see was ass that he slaps with pleasure. She starts to ride him rough, much like she does Thang who is heavy in her mind. Five is loving every minute of it watching her ass bounce up and down. He just grabs it by the handful and let go only to smack it which makes Faith moan in pleasure. They both reach a point in ecstasy in which they climax together and loud enough for someone on the other side of the door to hear.

Twurk and Thang finally made it to the Navi after running into some fans on their way out. "Yo bro, do you think that bitch with the strawberry streaks is worth fucking with man? Cause the way she was grinding on me, I know she wants the kid," inquired Thang. "Bro, you one wild ass dude you know that?" says Twurk as they both get in to leave. "Oh, don't act like I ain't seen you and that chick! You pulling one of your save-a-hoe stunts! You and that chick should have been in Hollywood acting or something with that scene y'all created," said Thang being all defensive about his situation. "Too bad I wasn't acting," Twurk said. The two of them start laughing as they pull out of the parking lot.

"So, I guess we're going to pay our two little friends a visit, huh?" asked Roc. "You know I keep my word!" said P-Murder looking at his crew who were ready for action. They arrived at the house and entered the dark basement room where the two were being held. The hostages stir as they hear footsteps coming down the stairs. "Are you two awake? Cause I have bad news for you, if you don't have good news for me!" yelled P-Murder. He slapped Juice across the face. "Do I make myself clear?" asked

P-Murder. Juice was always the most loyal to Money so he was not about to give him up even if they hadn't had eaten or drink any water in days. He said a prayer to himself because he knew he was risking death by not giving up the goods. "Fuck you, motherfucker!" Juice managed to weakly but defiantly bark back. P-Murder, although he admired the heart and loyalty Juice had, was about to show Juice why he was not to be played with. "Roc! Y'all take the lil nigga out back and dispose of him!" They grabbed Juice and removed him from the basement. "I hope you got better sense than your friend," P-Murder told Grillz. He didn't know what to do, but he knew he wanted to stay alive.

Outside Jitty could be heard saying, "It's grind time!" over and over again to taunt Juice, who refused to talk. "I hope you said your prayers!" said Reaper. "For this motherfucker to be about to die, he sure is quiet!" he added. They turned on the grinder, which made a loud sound. The sound is probably what made it real to Juice as to what was about to come next. He started struggling to get away but they managed to get him up on the platform then tossed him head first into the grinder. He screamed on the way down until he was silenced once and for all. His remains were collected on the other end in a big black hefty bag. They returned back inside carrying the hefty bag. "So, is he next?" Jitty asked P-Murder. "Chill, we have some people to go visit," P-Murder replied confidently. He lit up a blunt and they all went upstairs leaving the trash bag downstairs with Grillz. They all sat at the table to rest a bit. "Listen up!" P-Murder said trying to get everyone's attention. "We now have the drop on some major playas and they're moving some serious bread. So, we must move smart from now on. That means no hothead plays!" he said looking particularly at Heat.

At Twurk and Thang's house, mom had gotten up early to make them breakfast. Thang is awakened by the smell. After visiting the bathroom, he found his way into the kitchen. "Good morning, mom!" said Thang. "Good morning to you too!" she sung out in a harmonic voice. She was in a really good mood as she was humming while cooking. Twurk made his way into the kitchen next. He gave his mom a kiss on the cheek as he told her good morning and then took a seat across from Thang. "Mom, what's that song you're humming over there?" asked Thang. "It's definitely before your time!" said mom. She then turns to present to them two plates of pancakes and eggs cooked exactly the way each one of them prefers. "It feels so good to be back home and eating your cooking!" said Twurk. "Thanks son! I'm so glad to have you back with us!" she replied.

Pink and her crew are still in bed after the night they had. Peaches was having another bad dream and Pink heard her down the hall. In this dream, she is running from a two-headed dragon, but suddenly twists her ankle when she trips and falls. One of the heads on the dragon resembles Heat's face, the other she does not recognize but it unleashes a ball of blazing fire in her direction. Just before it hits her, she is awakened by Pink who had been trying to subdue all her kicking and swinging she was doing. Pink tried to calm her down by holding her as her breathing returned back to normal. She hugs Pink tightly as the dream scared her. "I'm right here Peaches! It's going to be ok" said Pink and they both went back to sleep.

In Choc and Strawberry's room, Choc was laid sprawled over Strawberry who was partly awake, and partly asleep but fully horny as she had been thinking about how big Thang's dick felt through his pants and how she loved the way she felt as she was grinding on him. Choc wakes up and asked Strawberry about how she slept because she had slept very well. She loved the way Strawberry looked in the morning. It turned her on. She placed her soft lips on Strawberry's nipples and playfully teased them with her tongue. She let her hands glide down Strawberry's stomach down in between her legs. Feeling how warm and wet she already was, just turned her on even more. She let her mouth follow her hands and proceeded to tease her clit just as she did her nipples. Strawberry starts winding her hips and grinding on Choc's face. Choc matches the friction with hard suction as if she was sucking up a thick milkshake. Strawberry starts to quiver as she comes multiple times. Choc tells her to turn over. "Arch that back!" she told Strawberry as she slapped her on the ass and gave her one or two good licks up the middle making sure to tease that clitoris even more. She pulled out one of her favorite vibrating toys. She places the pulsating head inside of Strawberry and begins to clap and toss her ass cheeks together repeatedly as they shook like bowls of jello. She uses her mouth to wiggle the toy around inside of her as well as thrusting it in and out. She did it to perfection just as one learns to play an instrument giving Strawberry multiple orgasms until she reached one final climax that caused her whole body to shake. She just collapsed unto the bed afterwards. Choc, very impressed by the work she just put in, crawled up to Strawberry's ear and whispers, "Who's pussy is this, boo" "It's yours, baby!" replied Strawberry all out of breath. "You damn right it is!" added Choc as she gave Strawberry one more smack on the ass.

At Five's place, he was getting ready to go to a meeting. "Baby, I'm on my way out. I love you!" he told Faith. He was running late as it was 7:15 am and he had a 45-minute drive to make an 8:00 meeting. He ran downstairs and out the door to the jag. Soon as she heard the car was far away she couldn't wait to call up the one she was longing for, Thang. She touched herself just thinking about him. She climaxed but decided she was unfulfilled and need Thang to finish the job. She called him on the phone. He was sitting around eating breakfast and talking to Twurk when he answered after recognizing her number. "Yo! What's up?" he asked after excusing himself from the table. "Mami needs papi right now!" "Damn! Do you know what time it is? Where is your nigga at?" asked Thang. "He left already so what are you going to do because I need you to come handle all of this," she said as she puts the phone between her legs so that he can hear how wet she was hoping that would make him come sooner and faster. "Give me a few and I'll be over there to pound that pussy out!" says Thang grabbing his manhood. "Hurry up!" she said as she went back to playing with herself.

Twurk and Thang left the house, but Twurk got dropped off by his father's gravesite. Thang, never goes there so he made plans to hit the road to go see Faith. "I'll be back later, while you do you. You know how I feel about this and dude!" Thang told

Twurk. "Yeah, I know! Don't take too long though!" said Twurk. Thang sped off to go see Faith. Before he could even get to the door to really knock on it, it swung open. Faith met him at the door wearing a black lace bra with matching panties. She jumps on him and wraps her legs around his waist while shoving her tongue down his throat.

He threw her onto the large soft leather couch and starts undressing quickly. He watches as she plays with herself in anticipation. She opens her legs and whispers to him, "Come get it, if you want it!" "I'm about to punish yo ass!" he said. "Promise?" she replied just before he thrusted himself inside her. Thang used the leverage of the couch to give her hard, deep thrusts. He started slow and deliberate at first, but then started to speed it up to give her just what she wanted. She screamed and moaned with pleasure from every stroke. "Ahh yeah! Fuck me papi! Fuck me harder!" she said just before she orgasmed. It only made her crave him more. She turned over to get in the doggy style position. "I hope that's not all you got! Give me more!" she said. "I want to feel you even when you're gone!" Thang knew he had to show and prove. He grabbed her by her long black hair and gives it a firm tug then he slapped both of her ass cheeks just to watch them jiggle and he knew it only made her wetter. He began to pound her out mercilessly and she loved every second of it as she threw it back with the same rhythm and aggressiveness. A perfect mix of pleasure and pain always did it for her as she reached her peak. Satisfaction was written all over her face. She laid her head on Thang's chest and looked up into his eyes as she thought of what it would be like being with him forever.

Chapter 13

Thang, on the other hand, was thinking of how Strawberry would feel if he was deep inside her. Faith starts gliding her hands up and down his chest and he knew exactly what her intentions were and where this was heading, so he placed his hand under her chin and raised her head up to look at him. The look on her face was saying she definitely wanted more. "Baby, I would stay longer, but I got some business to handle," he told her to escape the situation and he really did have to go since he left Twurk by the gravesite.

He made it to the cemetery just in time to see Twurk looking up at the sky as if he was talking to his father. "What a waste of time," he thought to himself. Twurk gets into the Navi and turns to Thang. "You know, it wouldn't hurt you to visit pops!" said Twurk. "What for, he's not there. I know where we're going to be at tonight though!" he said with a sneaky grin. "Where?" asked Twurk. "Club X.O.!" he replied as he turned the music up and pulled off.

P-Murder and his crew were posted outside of one of Money's spots waiting on Grillz to arrive. "Everything's clear my nigga!" said Grillz. P-Murder blew out a puff of smoke then says, "Good looking out my nigga. If things go according to plan, I might have a spot for you!" "When hell freezes over!" replied Grillz watching them pull off. To keep from being seen he pulled his hoodie over his head although his appearance is altered from the dirty clothes he was wearing and the now bushy hair he had developed while in captivity. He ducked off into the mini mart, while the crew pulled up to Money's spot wearing ski masks. "Let's go get it!" P-Murder tells his crew. The kicked down the door and go straight for the safe. They knew where it was located due to the info Grillz gave them. "Bingo!" said P-Murder as he opened the safe. "Don't leave nothing behind!" he tells them. "Execpt for our little parting gift!" he added with an evil grin. The parting gift, the black hefty bag, was left right in front of the safe.

When they made it back to their crib with one of the biggest payoffs of their lives, they divided up the task of weighing dope and counting the money. "Man! We fucking rich!" said P-Murder with a smile on his face. "Yo! P-Murder, we might need to smoke that lil nigga! He knows too much!" says Reaper. "This is the high life!" said Heat to himself. Roc rolled a blunt to celebrate.

Pink and her girls arrived back home from the mall. "I'm about to get ready!" said Pink as she took her bags to her room. Peaches went to her room and sat down on her bed. She started drifting off in her mind. She was on a yacht looking out to the sea of shiny blue waters leaned up against the rails. A red bird, the size of a crow with grayish, green eyes landed right beside her. She reached out to smooth its feathers but it flew away. Suddenly she was awakened by a knock at her door. "Come in!" said Peaches. "Girl, are you up for Club X.O. tonight?" asked Pink. "Sure, just give me some time to get ready!" she replied. "Good to have my Peaches back!" said Pink pinching her cheeks just before she left the room. Once ready, they all made their way to the club.

"This seems like a nice spot!" said Strawberry who was scoping every part of the perimeter. "Look! There's a good spot over there! Let's go sit there!" said Choc. They all made their way to the table. "All drinks on you tonight, right?" said Pink to Choc. "Yeah, girl! I know! I'll be back to quench your thirst!" she said as she made her way to the bar making sure to put an extra bounce in her step just in case anyone may be watching that might want to pick up the tab. Making her ass jiggle as she walked across the room usually did the trick because it was so huge that both men and women marveled at it. When she got to the bar, she ordered Moet for her and the girls. "What's good lil mama?" said a voice to her right. She turned to see that it was Thang. "What we sippin' on?" he asked. The bartender hands Choc the bottles she ordered. "Sorry, but these are for me and my girls!" she told him as she gave him a wink and turned around dramatically so he'd look at her ass as she walked away. She took pleasure in showing men something she didn't intend on giving them. Sure enough, his eyes followed her ass to their table but they also connected with Strawberry's eyes who was looking back at him. She could feel her desire for him getting stronger.

Twurk lets Thang know that he found a table for them and coincidentally it was not too far from the table where the girls were sitting. They leave the bar to go sit at the table. Soon as they sit down, Thang rolls up a blunt of loud and pours himself some red passion and takes a sip as he contemplated on how to get Strawberry. At the table with the girls, Pink is trying to get the girls to hit the dance floor. "I don't know about y'all but my song is on and I gotta get my groove on!" shouted Pink. "You always gotta get your groove on!" said Peaches as she laughed. "Come on boo! Let's get our groove on too!" said Choc pulling Strawberry to the dance floor. "You coming Peaches, or are you gonna sit and hold the table down?" asked Strawberry. "Girl! Y'all go and have some fun. I'll just watch y'all!" Peaches replied. Thang was watching as the girls made their way to the floor. "Watch my work, bruh!" said Thang cockily as made his way to the dance floor. He sneaks up behind Pink. Pink turns around suddenly. "Excuse me?" she said pointing a finger at him. "Can I have this dance pretty lady?" he replied. Since he asked so nicely and she wanted to get her groove on, she wrapped her arms around him and pulled him close. "I hope you can dance!" she added. They continued to dance as a slow song came over the speakers.

Watching her girls have fun on the dance floor and be happy, made Peaches happy. She took a sip from her drink. Out of nowhere came a familiar voice. "Excuse me miss! I saw you sitting by yourself and I was wondering if could join you?" She looked up to see a smile on Twurk's face. She smiled but didn't say anything. "Don't tell me cat got your tongue!" he teased. She laughed and said, "Yes, you may join me!" They talked for a little bit and laughed even more. "Would you like to dance?" asked Peaches. "I thought you'd never ask!" replied Twurk. They both made their way to the dance floor and he pulls Peaches in close. They embraced each other and Peaches laid her head on his chest. She could hear his heartbeat. This is one of those moments they had been waiting to share. They felt like they could dance in each other's arms all night.

Morning comes as Money and Pile-Up were still in Haiti getting ready to attend the burial ceremony of his father. Pile-Up gets a call on his phone. He excuses himself from the other gatherers to answer it. He returns with a grave look on his face that immediately alarms Money. "What is it?" he asked. "Word on the street is that some people hit your spot and they found Juice there, but it's not a pretty sight how they left him. They took everything in the safe and then some!" he reported. Put the word out, alarm the guerillas that there is hell to pay. Everyone involved must die! Money figured this had to be an inside job because only a handful of people knew where his safe was located and how to access it. He and Pile-Up made plans to be on the first private flight home that day after the ceremony.

They made it home just before dawn. Money took inventory of all the damage and disrespect to his property. It only made him even more angry when he saw where they left Juice's remains. One of his foot soldiers spotted Grillz at the court looking disheveled and trying to keep hidden so they made the call to report the sighting. "Get the guerillas and let's go!" Money told Pile-Up.

At the court Grillz was so caught up in his own thoughts about Juice and how he took the soldier's way out instead of being a coward like him, although he was thankful to be alive. He didn't notice at first when Money arrived at the scene nor when the guerillas started moving in his direction. Their orders were to take him alive because Money had special plans for him. What tipped him off is when others started to scatter and move out of the way as they knew something bad was going to go down. Grillz tried to make a fast getaway but to no avail. One of the guerillas shot him right in the leg which sent him tumbling to the ground. He was scooped up and put in the back of an SUV.

He was taken to another location but not before getting a beatdown on the way there. They brought him in and placed him in front of Money who had his dogs, Killa and Murda, on each side. He finally regained consciousness and looked through his good eye up at Money because the other was kind of swollen. "So, tell me something good Grillz!" was the first thing Money said to him. Terrified of what could come next, all he could mutter was "Yo! Money! I-I—" before he broke down crying. He would rather to still be in P-Murder's basement than where he is now.

Pile-Up walks in with a big black hefty bag and placed it in front of Grillz. "Open the bag!" Money told Grillz. Grillz couldn't move and didn't want to. "Now!" he insisted. Grillz crawled over to the bag while looking at Money with a face that begged for Money not to make him do this, but Money showed no remorse in his face at all. He opened the bag and what he saw remaining of his friend devastated him. "On the strength of Juice, I can get you P-Murder and his crew!" said Grillz knowing he owed a debt to Juice and it was his last card to play with Money. Hearing the name was confirmations to Money that he was on the right track to begin with. He was ready to do away with Grillz, but considered the offer because he did say everyone involved has to die. In order, to get everyone, he definitely needed Grillz to play his part. However, he wasn't going to let Grillz breathe that easily so he took a while to answer. He liked watching him squirm. "So ye know how to get dem, ye say?" asked Money. "Yes!" replied Grillz. "Ye better hope so!" said Money. Grillz let out a silent deep breath as his life was spared for the moment. Money walks up to the bag and pours out some coke. "You were loyal and served me well! I honor you and will look after your loved ones like dey are mine!" he said. "Make sure you dispose of the bag proper like!" he told Pile-Up. "Gather the men, I have a plan and take this one back to the hole, ye fix him up so dey are none the wiser," he added. One of the men, knocked Grillz unconscious before dragging him away.

P-Murder and his crew had decided to celebrate their score even more by throwing a big party. They had plenty of strippers and alcohol. It looked like one big frat party, with naked girls and they were doing stupid stunts like competing to see who can drink the most bottles in one sitting. They were making it rain on the strippers with the money they had stolen. Roc was especially enjoying himself as he went from receiving a lapdance to actually having sex with one of the strippers that had been eyeing him since they arrived. They were determined to make this a night to remember. P-Murder was receiving head from one of the strippers when he got interrupted by a phone call.

"Hello?" said P-Murder in an awkward voice because the stripper didn't stop when the phone rang. "What's up, man? This Grillz! I got something else for you!" "What is it?" he said stopping the stripper because he wanted to hear what Grillz had to say. "Meet me at the court!" said Grillz. "Bet! We'll be there!" said P-Murder. Grillz gave Money a head nod, signaling everything was set. "Let's go!" said Money to Pile-Up and the others.
P-Murder told the stripper he had to go handle some business but they should definitely get back up later.

Grillz, who was anxious to get this over with, spotted P-Murder and his crew pulling up, he pulls his hoodie down further to cover up the bruises as to not tip them off. Being in the shadows also aided him although he did walk with a slight limp due to being shot in the leg. Since, it was dark, it was hardly noticeable. They waited for Grillz to approach the vehicle while watching with a firm grip on their heaters to see if anyone was trying to sneak them in the process. Only Grillz showed up and to not take any chances, P-Murder just got straight to business. "So, where is it?" he asked Grillz impatiently. "Over on L-street. What's in for me this time? Last time I ain't get nothing!" said Grillz. "Ain't you still alive!" he replied while showing Grillz his uzi as he laughed. The rest of the crew laughed too and they pulled off to go get the goods.

Soon as they were out of sight, one of Money's men came from behind the bushes carrying a gun and told Grillz it's time to go. Grillz thought about running but the weapon made him change his mind.

Money, Pile-Up and the rest of the soldiers were lying in wait for P-Murder and his crew to make their move so they could make theirs. They didn't have to wait too long as they pulled up to the spot Grillz directed them too. "Looks like we're going to have an even better night!" P-Murder told his crew before they put on their ski masks. They check the perimeter and make their way to the location. They kick in the door and bumrush the place to get whatever they could get plus the stash. Soon as they were inside, Money's guerillas closed in on them. While inside, P-Murder and his crew came upon a huge stash of coke and so he tells Jitty to taste it. "Ugh! This shit tastes like—" Before he could finish his sentence the guerrillas burst through the door with their choppers ready to blaze up the place. "Ambush!" yelled P-Murder. Before Jitty could turn around enough to fire, he catches one to the head that pops it like a cheap balloon. His headless body fell to the grown. Reaper, now enraged, blazed on the first motherfucker he saw. He caught one between the eyes before he is riddled with bullets himself. Roc then took out two more of them before he is cut down himself. Watching his crew being mowed down like that caused him to panic. He started firing on any and everything moving, not caring if he lived or died. Heat shoots the remaining men but not before catching two shots to the body himself. He lands by Jitty's head.

Money gets impatient waiting for the men to come back out so he sends the lead guerilla in with Grillz in tow. P-Murder took in the scene around him and at his fallen crew until he heard footsteps coming in his direction. He hid behind this metal container that got tossed around the room early on. The guerilla entered the room, hemming Grillz up in front of him. Grillz was shaking like a leaf at being used like a shield and he didn't know what they would be walking into. P-Murder got the drop on the guerilla when he knelt down to say a prayer for his fallen comrades. Leaving only him and Grillz standing in the room.

P-Murder realized he should have listened to Reaper then none of this would have happened. "Motherfucker, you tricked us and expected to reap all the benefits, didn't you?" said P-Murder full of rage. "I didn't know man!" replied Grillz. "Walk!" he told

Grillz as he shoves him towards the front entrance. He intended to make Grillz his shield if someone tried to fire at him. When he saw no action, he took off sprinting towards the Hummer, leaving Grillz behind. When Money and Pile-Up saw no one coming from the house, they jumped out the ride and started bussin' but their shots only tore up the gravel and put a few holes in the Hummer. P-Murder managed to speed off and they got back in their SUV to follow him. Money was firing shots from the right backseat window to no avail.

P-Murder was speeding and swerving to get away from them and the barrage of bullets being hailed at him. He rounded the upcoming curve but in the wrong lane and hits a truck head on. P-Murder goes flying through the windshield leaving his upper body on the hood and the lower half still in the Hummer. The driver of the truck died instantly as the seatbelt decapitated him. The head landed on the hood of P-Murder's Hummer. They were face to face. Money and Pile-Up rolled up to the scene and saw the outcome of the accident. Thinking that there is no way he survived that, Money signals for him to just pull off. When no sound was heard and no lights were visible, P-Murder gathers himself and takes off through the woods. He was only knocked unconscious briefly which helped to make him appear to be dead. He was banged up and cut up but with no visible life-threatening injuries.

Money and Pile-Up made it back to the spot full of his fallen guerillas and P-Murder's fallen crew. "Torch de place! Too many bad memories!" he told Pile-Up. "Run me Grillz!" he added. Pile-Up takes a gas container from underneath the house and starts pouring it everywhere in the house. "May Jah be with ye!" he said before setting the house ablaze. After seeing the house truly catch on fire, they pull off. Inside, the flames were getting stronger and spreading rapidly. Lying on his back while being unable to move, Heat felt the flames catching on to his body at his feet and moving upwards. Realizing that, he is fucked at this point because he can't move, he faintly spits out "Peaches, you lucky bitch!" before screaming out in agony as the flames overtake him. Soon there is nothing but the sounds of the flames as the fire continues to burn.

Watching the fire burn from a spot tucked away, Grillz counted his blessings because he could just as easily have been burning too. It was still too early for him to breathe a sigh of relief as Money still wanted to take him out. "We still gotta get dat Grillz, Pile-Up! He is disloyal and bad news to our survival," said Money as he returned to his usual activity of inhaling lines of coke. Pile-Up placed a call to give the order that if anyone spots Grillz to put him six feet under.

Chapter 14

"Yo! What's good Thang!" asked Five when Thang answered the phone. "What it do Five?" replied Thang. "Tonight's the night for ya boy! You and your bro still with me?" he asked. "Of course, man! We wouldn't miss your bachelor party for nothing in the world!" "That's what it do man! You and your bro is like real family man! I'll see y'all later!" "Aight!" said Thang as he ended the call. "Who was that?" asked Twurk. "That was Five. His bachelor's party is tonight, remember?" replied Thang. "Oh yeah! That's right!" It had temporarily slipped Twurk's mind.

When it came time to get ready for the bachelor party, Twurk was the first to get dressed and ready of the two of them. Thang needed extra time. While he is getting dressed he spots a picture of him and Lola at the beach, which makes him think of their times together that they would never be able to share again. "You good bruh?" asked Twurk as he knocked on Thang's door. "Yeah! Come in bro!" "Everything aight bro?" asked Twurk again as he saw Thang handling the picture of him and Lola. "Yea bro! Everything's fine just give me a few more minutes," said Thang as he continues to get dressed. Twurk left the room and went into the living room where mom was sitting. "How are you mom?" asked Twurk as he sat beside her. "Im fine now that you're back with me, son! I've lost a lot of loved ones. I can't lose the two of y'all. You two are all I have left that mean that much to me!" she said as she looked him in the eyes. Twurk can see a mix of emotions in her eyes.

"You ready to go bruh?" asked Thang as he entered the room and then heads outside. "Don't worry mom, we'll be ok!" Twurk said as he bent down to give her a kiss on the cheek and walked towards the door. "Son, I'm never afraid when you're around" she said smiling at him. He flashes her a smile in return then closes the door behind him. Twurk and Thang made their way to Five's spot for the party. The parking area was packed with a lot of foreign whips in the mix. They finally found a spot to park and then headed inside. Five and the guys were seen having fun drinking and smoking as they walked in the door.

"What's up, man? Now this is what I'm talking about! My two main manz are here so let's get this party jumping!" shouted Five. The lights go dim then everybody takes a seat as a big cake is wheeled out on stage. "I guess the real party is about to begin!" says Thang with a grin on his face as he lights up a blunt. The music starts to play. It's "Body Party" by Ciara so they had an idea of what was to follow which makes the men get a bit rowdy.

Exotic women from various races start coming out of the cake dancing sensually. They start coming off the stage to the floor to dance up close for the men in the audience giving special attention and lapdances to the ballers who cops a feel as well as stuff their attire with money. The men were definitely enjoying the performance that the girls were putting on, but then the soft pink spotlights were shone on the cake and the music changed to "Salt Shaker" by the Ying Yang Twins. More women started coming out of the cake. Immediately, Twurk and Thang recognized the women as they emerged from the cake. Soon as Thang saw Pink and Strawberry all he could think about was pounding them both out. Twurk still couldn't believe his eyes as he saw Peaches come out of the cake. Peaches locked eyes with him and gives him a sexy smile as well as a look of lust in her eyes as she makes her way towards him. However, one of the men who had a little too much to drink blocked her path. She tied to evade him but it only made him more persistent. Twurk jumps up to go intervene.

"What's the matter bitch? My money ain't good enough for you, huh?" he asked aggressively while grabbing her arm. "Let go of me! You're hurting my arm!" she yelled back as she snatched away. She snatched away too hard and lost her balance. Seeing that she was about to fall Twurk rushed to catch her for the second time. Peaches looks up to see Twurk looking down at her. He helps her to regain her balance. She is embarrassed but grateful for Twurk as she holds on to him then begins to cry. Twurk puts his arm around her to comfort her and let her know she is safe now.

The drunk man is now burning with anger and envy at Twurk's intervention and tries to swing on him but missed. Even with Peaches in his arms he managed to evade the punch and comes back with one of his own sending the man to the ground. Twurk then picks him up and sits him down at a table like nothing happened. As far as the rest of the partygoers were concerned, nothing did happen. They were so captivated by the women and their seductive dancing. Pink saw Thang sitting at this table looking sexy and g'ed up. She seizes the moment and walks over to him. Thang watched out the corner of his eye as she came in his direction. Once she gets at his table, she straddles him and whispers in his ear, "You miss me?" as she starts riding him as if they were naked. He grabs her ass and replies, "You damn right!"

Strawberry saw them from across the room. She didn't like what she saw but she tried not to let it get to her as gives a lapdance to a baller with gold grillz. As his hands starts rubbing on her ass cheeks she starts grinding on him as if she was grinding on Thang. Choc gives Five a lapdance that makes him forget all about Faith for the moment. He is so drawn in by the sized and roundness of her ass that he feels like a kid in the candy store. "Do me good mami! Tonight is my last night as a free man!" he told Choc. She knew exactly what to do, but at first, she had to get the thoughts of a man touching all on her woman out of her mind. She was determined to give Five the best lapdance he ever had.

Thang, now really turned on by the dance he is receiving, whispers in Pink's ear if they could take it further because he was tired of being teased. "If your money 's right, of course. Not right here though!" she replied. Thang took Pink by the hand and led her to a private room where they begin to undress like they've been craving each other all along. Pink was so turned on to see how big Thang's dick was that she crawled on the bed in the room gripping the satin sheets assuming doggy style position with a deep arch in her back. She looked back at him biting her bottom lip. "Come give mami what she needs!" she said seductively. Thang gets so turned on by the view of her round ass and juicy lips that were glistening from how wet she already was. He makes his way toward the bed and without warning thrusts his massive manhood inside her, which made her arch even more as she feels him creeping towards her stomach.

He grabs a handful of her hair as she begs for him to give her the satisfaction she's been waiting for. "Careful what you ask for, 'cause you just might get it all!" he whispered in her ear. "Fuck me, damn it! Fuck me now!" Pink demands. He keeps giving her deep thrusts as her juices run down his legs. She enjoyed the pain and the pleasure Thang was giving her. She only seemed to get wetter with each stroke and especially when she climaxed with two strong orgasms. She starts throwing it back extra aggressively as she prepares for her third orgasm which seemed bigger than the last two. She couldn't let out a scream this time, but a single tear managed to escape her right eye. Thang came a few seconds afterwards.

Outside, Twurk still held Peaches close to him while looking deep into her eyes. The chemistry between them is obvious. They are in their own world, one in which Peaches feels free and doesn't want the moment to end. She wanted to show him her appreciation for coming to her rescue all those times. "Can we go somewhere more private?" Twurk asked. "What do you have in mind?" she asked. A slow song plays in the background, "Love Song" by Rihanna and Future. The lyrics of the chorus filled his heart and mind so he just went with the flow. He leans into Peaches and kisses her. She kisses him back as his hands slides down the small of her back and rests on her ass under her two cheeks. He had been waiting on this moment for a while. His kisses send shockwaves through her mind, body, and soul. Before long, they are grinding on each other. She is getting wetter and wetter and can feel a pulsating sensation between her legs. She wanted him badly. He noticed that they are breathing a bit harder and she is starting to moan softly so he suggested that they go to his truck. She is on the same page.

Once outside they make their way to the Navi and he opens the door for her to let her inside. Soon as he gets inside, she goes straight for his zipper then pull down his pants and boxers. She grabs his erect manhood and leads him between her legs. She used the tip to slide her thongs to the side and helped to guide all of Twurk inside her. He pulls her to the edge of the seat and wraps her legs around his neck. "Promise me you won't hurt me cause I'm falling in love with you!" she told him. He replied that he felt the same. Peaches was glad to hear that he felt the same and it made the sex even more pleasurable. She asked him to switch positions so she can ride him like she fantasized. Twurk relaxed as she straddled him and begin to wind and grind her hips as well as bounce up and down. She also did a gradual 360-spin as she rode him in different positions. Her favorite position was reverse cowgirl. She could feel all of him. He enjoyed it even more as her juices flowed all over him and she moaned loudly with pleasure as he played with clit to make her have an intense orgasm. Just as she had made her way back around to face Twurk she could feel it coming so she spread her legs as far apart as she could to drive Twurk deeper inside her. Her body started to quiver as she let out a loud high-pitched scream as they orgasmed together. She laid on Twurk's chest when it was all done. The night ended with a bang for Twurk and Thang.

The next day, Peaches called Thang to see what he was doing? She got wet just thinking about how they fucked in the back of his Navi. "I'm not doing much at the moment but the day is full of possibilities, you know?" said Twurk. "Can I com scoop you up?" he asked. "You can come in about an hour" she said. "Well, I'll see you in about an hour then" he said before sending Peaches kisses through the phone.

Pink lay in her bed still feeling the effects of the sex she had last night with Thang. She smiled when she thought of all the pleasure so she decided to call him. Thang recognized the number soon as it popped up on his phone. He smiled because he knew she'd be calling for more of what he gave her last night. "Hello!" he answered. "Good to hear your voice, so what' s good?" she asked. "You and me, I hope!" he replied while flexing in the mirror naked. "You know, after last night, my pussy is calling your name!" she said as she let out a soft moan. "Can I see you tonight?" he asked. "How does 9:00 sound?" "Bet! I'll see you at 9!" he said before ending the call. Pink couldn't wait to feel Thang inside her. Just the thought of it made her so wet. She had always told herself, that she'll never get caught up with another man, but for Thang, she was willing to risk it all.

Twurk came to Thang's door. "Bro, I'm about to be out for a while!" "Aight, but I got some business to handle before 9:00, though," replied Thang. Twurk, left to go pick up Peaches. Once outside the house, he honked the horn to let Peaches know he was outside. She opens the door to come out. He gets out the ride to greet her and open the door for her. He admired her beauty and her sexiness as she walked towards him. He opened the passenger door. She gives him a surprise kiss on the cheek then gets in the Navi. Twurk closes the door and heads to the driver's side to get in. He puts on "I want to be your man" by Zapp & Roger. "What you know about that?" asked Peaches as she giggled a little. "I know enough to let you know that it's the kind of grown & sexy music that people who know what and who they want in life listens to," he replied while looking into her eyes. She sensed the sincerity in his tone as she glared back at him. "Let's go see a movie!" "Aight!" she replied.

Once they get to the theater, Twurk buys some popcorn and sodas before they go in to find their seats. The lights go out and then the movie starts. Twurk takes this opportunity to put his arm around her. Peaches smiles at him and leans in closer. They watched the movie while eating the popcorn they shared and fed to each other. After it was over, they looked at each other and shared a passionate kiss. "That was a great movie!" said Peaches as they walked toward the Navi hand in hand. "So, do you believe in happy endings?" he asked her. "If it's with the person you love, then yes," she replied before they kissed again.

When they arrived back at Peaches' house, they turned to look at each other. "Well! I had a good time today! I'm definitely looking forward to spending more time with you," said Peaches. Twurk puts his hand on the side of her face and brushes away a single strand of hair. "Did you mean what you said earlier about happy endings?" he asked. "Yes!" she replied as her heart begin to race with anticipation. "Cause I'm happy with you and want you to stay in my life," he told her before they share a kiss that melts her heart and soaks her panties at the same time. She told Twurk goodbye and headed into the house. Twurk headed home to chill and let Thang use the Navi.

Twurk finally made it home to see Thang waiting on the front porch. "It's about time bro, I thought I was going to have to send out a search party or something!" said Thang as Twurk tossed him the keys. "Later bro!" said Twurk then he went inside.

Pink, who couldn't wait to see Thang, was in her room lost in her thoughts. She didn't even notice Choc standing in her doorway. Choc watched as she was dancing to Juvenile's "Back that Ass Up" and begins to feel the rhythm herself so she started dancing along with her. She actually starts to mimic Pink's dancing in a joking way. Pink finally turns around to see Choc and almost jumps out of her skin. "You scared me girl! How long you been standing there?" Choc laughed. "Long enough to know that you've been dickmatized and I do believe that your ride is out there," she replied as she walked off. She was thinking that it was better that Thang was here for Pink rather than Strawberry.

Pink rushes downstairs and out the door. She reaches the Navi to see Thang looking back at her on the driver's side. She opened the door to get inside. Thang was checking her out as she did, admiring her sexiness. From inside the house Strawberry was watching through the window with envy. "You may have him now, but once I put this pussy on him, he's going to be mines," she thought to herself. Just then, Choc comes in the room with nothing on. She has a spray can of whip cream in one hand a pair of handcuffs in the other. "Ready for a little dessert?" she asked Strawberry.

"You smoke?" Thang asked Pink as he lit up a blunt of loud. "No! Not really, but…." "You do or you don't?" he asked as he cut her off mid-sentence. Pink was a little annoyed by this. "Well damn!

Who done pissed you off 'cause I didn't come for no shitty ass mood!" replied Pink. "What are you here for then?" he asked just to see where she's at in her line of thinking. Pink didn't want Thang to see her emotions so she just looked out the window. Knowing he struck a nerve, he looks over at her and smiles. He pulls up to the drive through and asks her if she's hungry. "No! I've lost my appetite! "she said in an irritated tone. He tries to touch her face and she swipes his hand away. She looks at him now almost to the point of tears and asked him why does he hurt her. He wipes away a tear with his fingertip then said to her, "If I can't hurt you, then I can't love you!" in his sincerest voice possible.

With those words Pink became speechless. She closed her eyes as she received the most electrifying kiss that she'd ever had. For a minute, they forgot they were in the drive thru line so they had a bit of an audience watching. All the whistling and applauding they heard is what made them remember. They looked at each other and laughed. "So, what do you want to eat?' he asked. "Whatever you're having!" she replied as the kiss sent her brain into a bit of a frenzy and she couldn't think straight.

After they got their food, he pulled over to a private spot in the parking area so they could eat. He starts to devour his food and Pink could only watch in amazement at how he was eating. "What?" he said as he caught her looking at him. She shook her head and continues to eat her own food. When they were finished, Pink wiped the corners of her mouth with her napkin but she turned to look at Thang who was about to use his sleeve. "Don't you dare! This is how you should do it!" said Pink as she gently wiped the sauce from his face. Seeing that she had this kind of care for him turned him on. He pulled her in close and kissed her passionately. "Hold up! Not right here!" she said as she gently pulled away. She didn't want to start anything they wouldn't be able to finish. He realized what she meant and came to an agreeance. He gathered their wrappings to throw them in the trash. "Gotta keep the Navi clean!" said Twurk. He came back with the idea of getting a suite at a hotel so they can have some privacy and finish what they started. Pink was definitely with it, so they made their way to the closest one they could find.

Once in the room, they started their prior physical conversation soon as they crossed the threshold. They took off each other's clothes before making their way to the bed. Thang stared Pink in her eyes as he pinned both her legs up by her head and dives deep into her wetness. Stroke after stroke, she moaned and screamed. She only appeared to get wetter and wetter until she climaxed. "I ain't done yet, ma!" he said flipping her over into doggy style position. "Arch that back!" he demanded as he gripped her waist before pounding her out mercilessly. He gave her multiple orgasms until they he achieved a big one. They were both out for the count as they fell asleep in each other's arms.

The next morning Thang enters the house after dropping off Pink. "Good morning to you too!" his mom said giving him a look that doesn't need to be explained. "Oh, mom! Don't start that with me this morning!" replied Thang a little annoyed. She stood there looking at him in disbelief, then turns to walk off. He snuck up behind her, wrapped his arms around her while scooping her off her and spun her around. "Gotcha now!" he told her as he laughed. "Good morning mom and just know that I love you always!" he said as he placed her back on her feet. After she composed herself from the dizziness, she replied with "I love you too, son!" "Who got you going early this morning?" "Life!" he replied as he walked to his room. Mom said a silent thankful prayer and finished cooking breakfast.

Twurk came in the kitchen to get a bite to eat as he smelled his mom's cooking all the way in his room. As he was enjoying breakfast, his phone rung. "Hey handsome!" said the voice on the other line. It was Peaches calling to let him know she was thinking of him. "So, what's on your agenda for today?" she asked. "My man Five is getting married today at 5!" he replied with a smile thinking that could one day be him. "Who is the best man?" "My bro and I are both best men in the wedding" "Okay, I know you're going to look great in your suit!" said Peaches. "Give me a call later and wish the bride and groom luck for me!" she said before they ended the call.

Twurk and Thang arrived at Five's house a few hours before the wedding. As they entered the doorway they immediately see Five and Red. Together they look like they were a part of the red mafia in their customized and highly tailored red suits. They all dapped each other up and the twins especially gave a brotherly hug to Five. "Today is our lucky day, ain't it?" Thang said to Five. "Yeah, man! It's finally here!" he replied. "Five, I wish you all the best brother!" said Twurk.

In another room of the house, Faith sat upright looking elegantly while getting for the wedding. For a moment, she was just staring into the vanity's mirror as her girls work quickly to help with the preparations for the day. "Faith, you look so beautiful! I wish I were you! You got a fine ass rich man, a huge beautiful house and I can only imagine what else! What more could you possibly want?" said one of her girls helping with her hair. Faith only smiled in agreeance, but in the back of her mind she knew she still lacked the one thing Thang gave to her. Just the mere thought of him sends shockwaves through her body that all seem to go straight to her spot that pulsates and breaks the dam that allows her wetness to overflow. That's what she didn't have with Five.

When it was time for the ceremony to begin, everyone gathered outside in their seats. Five and his two best men were down front waiting for the wedding party to make their way down the aisle before it was time for the bride to come. After the last bridesmaid and groomsmen came down everyone stood up for the moment when the bride comes. The ceremonial music starts to play to introduce the bride. Five could hardly stand still as he anticipated this very moment for a long time. He watched with a smile on his face as the most beautiful woman he had ever seen came walking down the aisle towards him. He was definitely not the only man watching though.

The preacher starts the ceremony. They both had written their own vows that they said to each other. Thang was looking directly at Faith as she said her vows to Five and she looked at Five in a way that she also could see Thang's face. After they said their vows and "I do's" they were pronounced husband and wife. "You may now kiss your bride!" the preacher told Five as the audience applauded and the music played. In Thang's mind, he saw Faith but her face briefly flashed to every woman he has messed with including Lola, Strawberry and finally Pink saying "I do" before returning back to Faith. He closed his eyes and shook his head a bit to regain his focus.

After the wedding ceremony was over, it was time for the bride and groom to depart. Thang watched as Five and Faith's head off to get inside a red stretch limo that will take them to the airport in order for them to go on their honeymoon. Despite how he feels, he is smiling, thinking to himself, "have fun, playboy!" "I'm so happy for the two of them!" said Red. Twurk was thinking about Peaches the whole time while watching Five and Faith ride off in the limo.

Later that evening as Twurk and Thang were riding around when the alert went off on their phones at the same time. Pink had text Thang and Twurk received a text from Peaches. They receive the same text inviting them to Club XS. Twurk texted back "Club XS it is. I'll see ya there!" and Peaches replied with a "xoxo". "What the hell is Club XS?" Thang asked Twurk as he laughed. He texted the same to Pink. "Are you coming or what? Cause I want to spend some time with you," Pink replied. "If my bro coming then I'll go." "What? You didn't need him the other night, did you?" Pink replied back. "No, I didn't...mmhmm...I'll see you there!"

Pink and her girls arrived first. They sat outside the club in their Lexus waiting on Twurk & Thang. Choc seemed a little impatient waiting on them but it was solely because of Thang's interaction with Strawberry at the bachelor party. Strawberry only pretended to be impatient to be in agreeance with Choc and to not let on that she was still feeling Thang. Twurk & Thang arrived a twenty minutes later. Pink and Peaches were happy to see them. Pink walked up to Thang and wraps her arms around his neck. "I'm glad you kept your word!" she said in his ear. Twurk met Peaches halfway and she gives him a kiss on the lips and a hug. Strawberry looks at Thang and Pink out of the corner of her eyes longing to be the one close to him. They finally make their way inside the club, which was packed to capacity. After weaving through the crowd, they finally found a table to sit down. Twurk and Thang offered to go get the ladies some drinks. They went to the bar to order 4 bottles of Moet and 2 bottles of Red Passion.

"Aight, give me some help here!" said Thang. Strawberry was too happy to do so as she deliberately grazed his hand while making eye contact as she is reaching for the two bottles of Moet. She quickly hands one to Choc who didn't notice a thing. "Y'all welcome!" he said to Choc and Strawberry sarcastically. "Damn! Where's my manners today? Thank you boo!" said Choc looking over Strawberry. "Thanks! Twurk, you're so generous!" said Pink trying to prevent a clash from happening. "Here boo, let me pop that top for you!" says Choc to Strawberry. Twurk opens Peaches' bottle and pours her a glass and then pour himself a drink from his bottle.

They all sipped and talked amongst each other until Twurk heard an old slow jam that he liked. He grabs Peaches by the hand. "Come dance with me!" he said. She got up and they made their way to the dance floor. They moved in close to each other as she laid her head on his chest. She could hear his heartbeat as they swayed to the music. "I'm in love with you!" Twurk whispered in Peaches' ear. She looked at him in the eyes and smiled as this was her feelings for a long time now. "I'm in love with you too!" she replied as they continued to dance. Thang and Pink had made their way to the floor and Pink is making sure to get extra close to Thang. He grips her waist then moves down to grip her ass as she wrapped her arms around him tightly. "Do you love me?" she asked. Thang was a little gone off the blunts and the red passion and he was definitely infatuated with her ass. He was fumbling around and didn't know what to say as he avoided looking at her and somehow locked eyes with Strawberry. "Yeah!" he said hurriedly but with deception. He just didn't want to upset her or run the risk of not getting any. She held on to the moment as she held on to him. They danced and drank until it was closing time and they parted ways.

The next day as Thang is sleeping off the drinks and blunts he had the night before, he is awakened by his phone. He didn't recognize the number. "Who's this?" he said sleepily when he answered the phone. "Can I see you today? My girls are going to the mall and I'm going to play sick so you can come through and get some of this strawberry," she said taunting him. By now he was fully awake and knew exactly who it was on the other end. Although he was a bit conflicted after being with Pink, he had been waiting to hear these similar words for a while. "What time?" he asked. "Come around 2:00 and don't be late!" "You just make sure you be good and ready to take all this d—" She had hung up before he could finish because Choc came in the room. Thang got up, took a shower, and then got dressed.

Pink and the other girls finally leave the house to go to the mall, while Strawberry stayed behind. Moments later, Thang pulled up outside. He walked up to the door and knocked. "Come in big daddy!" said the voice on the other side. He walked inside to find a naked Strawberry waiting with a lustful look in her eyes as she stared at what she wanted the most. He closes the door behind him. She motions for him to come closer as she planted a wet kiss on his lips. He smacked her on the ass before picking her up and carrying her upstairs to her room. He then threw her down on the bed which she covered with silk sheets soon as Choc left. He quickly took off his clothes while watching her play with herself and squeeze her nipples. Before he could get on the bed she crawled over to him admiring the sized of his dick before swallowing it. She ran her wet mouth and tongue up and down the shaft, making sure to not leave his balls out of the fun. She did it so good that she drove Thang crazy as he dropped his head back and grabbed the back of her head. She slowly releases him from her mouth but gives him one last good lick from shaft to tip before lying on her back to welcome him inside the land of Strawberry.

She is lying spread eagle as he climbs on top of her and slowly puts the tip in, teasing her. Then roughly jams it all the way in just to hear the sound she'd make. It turned him on and her as well. "Remember, this is what you asked for!" he told her before pushing one of her legs up by her head. He makes sure to give her strong, deep thrusts that went from slow, to mid-tempo and then he picked up the pace. She was trying to hold on to the headboard as to not go through it with the way he was beating it. He kept hitting her g-spot so every now and then she would squirt. All the wetness just turned him on even more and made him go harder. She never knew she could feel punished and this pleased at the same time. Seeing how wet Strawberry was, he wanted to get the best view, so he told her to get on her knees in the doggy style position. He admired the view from back as he smacked her ass cheeks which made her squirt a little. "Damn! I'm about to punish this good ass pussy!" he said. He spread her cheeks apart and slowly slid inside as to not cum to quickly. Once he gathered himself and found his rhythm again he picked back up to the same rhythm as before but more pronounced. He liked the way her ass jiggled as he made contact. His relentless strokes made her scream out in pleasure and have an orgasm that seemed to last forever. As hers ended his had just began. They both lay in the bed, now breathing heavily and sweating from all the activity. "Damn! That was so good daddy!" she said. "You damn right!" he replied in a cocky manner. Thang, didn't want to get caught slippin' so he didn't lie around too long before he got and got dressed to head home. Strawberry blew him a kiss as he left the room.

Thang pulled into the driveway with the music playing loud. Twurk steps out on the porch when he heard the music. Thang gets all smiling like a Cheshire cat and looing lively. "What's good, Playa?" Twurk asks. "The world I live in!" he answered back feeling himself. "I never felt so alive in my life bruh!" Twurk was glad to see his brother in good spirits.

The girls return back home from shopping at the mall. Choc runs in the house and towards the room. "Baby! Look at what I got for you!" she yelled. She found Strawberry still lying in the bed with her favorite blanket pulled up to her neck sleeping peacefully. "Oh! My bad boo!" she said as she startled Strawberry who slightly opened her eyes. "Can I get you anything, boo?" asked Choc. "No! I'm good. I just need some rest," said Strawberry. She was near comatose from her sexual rendezvous with Thang. Now she understood what made Pink change her cold heart because even though she clearly loved the fine and voluptuous Choc, she still wanted Thang, badly.

Chapter 15

Five was enjoying his time with Faith on their honeymoon. He stood looking out at the ocean from their room window as he watched the birds fly freely around the beautiful sky. As the sun set, he took a sip of brandy as he thought about how good his life has been thus far. Faith sneaks up behind him and embraces him to caress his abs and chest. He loved her so much that her touch sent sensations throughout his body giving him an instant hard-on. She kissed the back of his neck as she put her hands down his boxers gripping the very thing she wanted him to give her. "Come back to bed papi!" she whispered in his ear.

Five quickly turned around and lifts Faith off her feet. The two of them start kissing wildly and passionately. He carried her back to the bed and removed her thong. She braced herself as Five kissed her navel and worked his way down to her lips, which he parted with his tongue to reveal her clit. His mission was to please and he made it clear as he teased, licked and sucked until her legs started to quiver. She tried to run from it but he gripped her waist to hold her in place. She dug into the bed's silk sheets as she lets out screams and moans of pleasure. Five made sure to also lick all of her nectar with each orgasm then proceed to give her another one. After the fifth one, she lets out an ear-splitting scream that the neighbors probably heard. Five releases his grip and gives her one final suck and a wet sloppy kiss. Faith curled up into fetal position, satisfied. While she was pleased to find out that Five had the ability to please her, in the back of her mind she still longed-for Thang. She listened to the sound of the ocean as she drifted off to sleep.

STAY TUNED............

MORE TO COME FROM
THE
TWURK & THANG SERIES

Contact Author Frank Zeigler Jr:

AuthorNittyz@gmail.com

Website: Coming Soon!

Address for fanmail:

Frank Zeigler Jr #311279 EB #176
PO Box 252
Turbeville, SC 29162

NEW BOOKS COMING SOON!!!